JACOB WONDERBAR

for president of the universe

nathan bransford

illustrated by
C.S. Jennings

DIAL BOOKS
FOR YOUNG READERS
an imprint of penguin group (usa) inc.

DIAL BOOKS FOR YOUNG READERS
A division of Penguin Young Readers Group
Published by The Penguin Group
Penguin Group (USA) Inc., 375 Hudson Street, New York, NY 10014, U.S.A.
Penguin Group (Canada), 90 Eglinton Avenue East, Suite 700, Toronto,
Ontario, Canada M4P 2Y3 (a division of Pearson Penguin Canada Inc.)
Penguin Books Ltd, 80 Strand, London WC2R 0RL, England
Penguin Ireland, 25 St. Stephen's Green, Dublin 2, Ireland
(a division of Penguin Books Ltd)
Penguin Group (Australia), 250 Camberwell Road, Camberwell, Victoria 3124,
Australia (a division of Pearson Australia Group Pty Ltd)
Penguin Books India Pvt Ltd, 11 Community Centre,
Panchsheel Park, New Delhi - 110 017, India
Penguin Group (NZ), 67 Apollo Drive, Rosedale, Auckland 0632,
New Zealand (a division of Pearson New Zealand Ltd)
Penguin Books (South Africa) (Pty) Ltd, 24 Sturdee Avenue, Rosebank,
Johannesburg 2196, South Africa
Penguin Books Ltd, Registered Offices: 80 Strand,
London WC2R 0RL, England

Book design by Jasmin Rubero
Text set in Breughel Com
Printed in the U.S.A.

1 3 5 7 9 10 8 6 4 2

Library of Congress Cataloging-in-Publication-Data
Bransford, Nathan.
Jacob Wonderbar for President of the Universe /
Nathan Bransford ; illustrated by C. S. Jennings.
p. cm.
Summary: When seventh grader Jacob Wonderbar is nominated for President
of the Universe, he and his best friends Sarah Daisy and Dexter take off for
outer space to campaign, and in the process suffer kidnappings, space monkeys,
dirty politics, and threats to blow up the Earth.
ISBN 978-0-8037-3538-5 (hardcover)
[1. Interplanetary voyages—Fiction. 2. Politics, Practical—Fiction.
3. Adventure and adventurers—Fiction.] I. Jennings, C. S., ill. II. Title.
PZ7.B73755Jaf 2012
[Fic]—dc23

chapter 1

Jacob slammed the door to his mom's car and stomped through the supermarket parking lot.

"Jacob," his mother called after him. "I can understand if you don't want to talk about it, but please don't take it out on my car."

On the ride to the store, Jacob had deflected his mom's incessant questions through a surprisingly effective combination of staring out the window and grunting. As far as he was concerned, there was nothing to talk about. His dad was out of his life, and one more tally on a long list of broken promises didn't change anything.

After receiving a wrinkled postcard from his dad a few weeks back saying that he would be in town and wanted to take Jacob to lunch, Jacob spent the appointed morning staring out the window, waiting for his dad long past the time he had promised he would arrive. Jacob's excitement had changed to impatience to annoyance to anger and finally to resignation. Four hours later he had given up and felt silly for even believing his dad would show up in the first place.

One postcard and one more no-show didn't change anything. He would wake up again the next morning, and his dad would still be gone, he still wouldn't be a part of his life, and there was nothing in the world that Jacob could do about it.

"Hey," his mom said, catching up to him. She handed him a list. "Grab these things for me and you can pick out something for yourself."

She put her arm around him and he actually didn't mind the hug, though he looked around quickly to make sure there wasn't anybody from school who saw it.

Jacob walked slowly around the giant supermarket, picking up the tomatoes, canned tuna, and sugar on his list, thinking about what he wanted for himself. Jerky? Corn Pops? Chocolate milk? Wasabi peas? But when he made it to the frozen foods aisle, he knew exactly what he was craving.

A prank.

It came to him in a flash. He would convince the

supermarket manager that corndogs came from chickens with wooden legs.

He found the corndog section, opened the freezer door, felt the rush of cold on his face, and grabbed a box.

"Psst!" he heard from inside the freezer.

Jacob peered in between the clear plastic sheets that lined the back of the freezer. He saw something move.

"What are you doing here?" the voice said. It wasn't the manager, but someone more peculiar.

An eye peeked through. Jacob forgot about his prank and slammed the freezer door. He wondered if he should tell his mom that a creepy supermarket employee was spying on his frozen food choices.

Down the aisle, the door to the freezer opened and Jacob saw someone emerge. For a fleeting moment he thought it might be his dad, that a message had gone awry and it had been a misunderstanding, but instead he saw that it was the man in silver, who had once given him a spaceship and set his space adventures in motion. Jacob ran over and they ducked into the freezer.

He looked around at stacks of pizza boxes and TV dinners and bags of meat in blue plastic crates. The man in silver was holding a half-eaten corndog.

"You eat them frozen?!" Jacob asked.

The man in silver cocked his head. "They're pre-cooked. What are you doing at the supermarket? Haven't you heard the news? The king has called elections and he has nominated you for president of the universe!"

"President?" Jacob rubbed his arms, which were getting very cold. "Shouldn't they get an adult to do that?"

The man in silver looked horrified. "An adult? Oh my, Jacob, that is a terrible idea. Adults just want to stand around and talk, and . . . Could you imagine the speeches? Ugh." He shivered. "I hope you will not be

making decisions like that once you are in office."

Jacob couldn't imagine being in charge of the universe. He didn't even know where all the different planets were, and last time he couldn't even fly around space without blowing up some stars, causing a giant space kapow, getting stuck on a planet of substitute teachers, and barely escaping with his life. Being able to fly around the universe without destroying it was probably a rather basic part of the president's job description.

"What about the king?" Jacob asked. "What's happening to him?"

"No one knows. But listen, there isn't much time left. You have to make it to Planet Headline to declare your candidacy in . . ." The man in silver looked at a small piece of plastic. "Less than six zoomecs."

"What's a zoomec?"

"Forty-seven parcelticks."

Jacob blinked in confusion. "Huh?

The man in silver waved impatiently. "You have about two Earth days. Are you going? You'd better hurry."

Jacob imagined blasting off into space and giving speeches and shaking hands with Astrals and possibly having control over everything. He certainly had some ideas about reducing the number of vegetables

children were forced to consume, and there were some laws regarding fatherhood that he wouldn't mind enacting. He wasn't really sure that he was cut out to be a politician, but if the king had confidence in him . . .

"I'm in. Where's the spaceship?"

The man in silver took a bite out of his corndog and frowned. "How am I supposed to know?" he said with his mouth full. "You took mine last time and you didn't even bring it back. I've been stuck on this planet ever since."

chapter 2

After coming home from the grocery store, Jacob wanted to call Sarah and Dexter immediately to tell them about the man in silver, but his mother insisted on their usual Sunday Family Bonding Night, the rules of which were strict and exacting: No phone calls, texting, e-mails, or other distractions were permitted, and talking about what happened during the previous week was strongly encouraged. Jacob kept his mom company while she cooked a meal large enough to result in leftovers for the rest of the week, and after eating they always sat down to watch a movie together, although inevitably his mom would fall asleep on the couch and Jacob would end up watching the movie by himself.

His mom didn't make it through the first fifteen minutes of *The Iron Giant* before she started snoring, and Jacob thought about sneaking out of the house to run over and tell Sarah and Dexter about the election, or at least sneak in a few text messages. But getting himself into trouble with his mom wasn't something Jacob could risk. He didn't imagine that the public responded favorably when presidential candidates were grounded by their parents. He needed a better plan.

There couldn't have been many zoomecs remaining before the deadline when Jacob awoke on Monday morning and rushed to school. He arrived a few minutes early, and when he opened the door he saw Dexter studying alone in the classroom. Jacob still hadn't gotten used to how much taller Dexter had grown lately. It was almost as if his parents put him through a stretching machine every morning to make him a few inches taller and a few inches skinnier.

"There you are . . ." Jacob said.

He handed Dexter one of his most valuable possessions, an immensely precious item that somehow only cost $9.99 plus shipping and handling, which he had charged to his mother's credit card when she wasn't paying attention.

Dexter looked at the label. "Sneezing powder? Oh no . . . No no no . . ."

"Dexter, the man in silver . . ."

Sarah walked into the room, staring at her cell phone. She was still wearing her shin guards from before-school soccer practice, and her face was red and sweaty. "Jake, is this true?"

Dexter's parents had not allowed him to get a cell phone, in order to instill in him an appreciation for older forms of communication, like writing letters and getting out of your chair and walking down the street when you had something to say to someone. Unfortunately, this meant he was always the last one to know about everything. "What about the man in silver?" Dexter asked.

Jacob beamed. "The king nominated me for president of the universe!"

He had expected congratulations, but Dexter and Sarah just looked extremely confused.

"You?" Dexter asked. "No offense, but are you sure you're . . . you know . . ." He held up the sneezing powder. "Presidential material?"

Sarah scowled. "Of course they'd nominate a boy. Of course they would."

"Sarah . . ."

"The king doesn't think I'm qualified to be president? You know what that is? That's gender discrimination!"

Jacob snatched the sneezing powder back from Dexter. He should have known they wouldn't think he could do it. "Fine," he said. "I guess I'll just have to prove my own friends wrong."

Sarah and Dexter looked at each other and then back at Jacob. He started to storm out of the room.

Sarah took a deep breath and she caught Jacob's hand as he walked by her. Jacob noted that it was the second and a half time they had ever held hands. "Sorry, Jake. Um. Congratulations."

Dexter pointed at the sneezing powder. "Congratulations and everything, but really, what's that for?"

Jacob let go of Sarah's hand. "We need to find a spaceship quickly because we don't have that much time left before I have to announce that I'm running. Subs must fly to Earth on spaceships, right? We find ourselves a substitute teacher and then we steal their spaceship. That's the plan."

"Okay . . ." Dexter said. "But we haven't had a substitute all year. And Mr. Kruger doesn't get sick. He won't even shake anyone's hand without using hand sanitizer."

Jacob held up the sneezing powder. "Exactly."

It was twenty minutes later when the first seventh grader sneezed. Mr. Kruger looked up from his roll sheet. "Robbie, please remember to always sneeze into your arm and . . ."

Robbie sneezed again. Mr. Kruger took a step backward. "Young man? Do you need to see the nurse?"

There were three more sneezes around the classroom and Mr. Kruger began retreating toward his desk for hand sanitizer. Soon there was a cascading of sneezes and Jacob felt tears in his eyes as he began sneezing as well.

"Sneeze into your arms!" Mr. Kruger yelped. "Sneeze into your arms!"

Sarah raised her hand and then spoke up over the mass sneezing. "Mr. Kruger, I saw this on WebMD! There was an alert about a deadly bird virus and the symptoms are sneezing and vomiting!"

The entire plan depended on Dexter. After several traumatizing periods of PE, Dexter had perfected the art of vomiting on command. Whenever he couldn't bear the thought of changing clothes in front of eighth-grade Neanderthals he would ask to be excused from class because he wasn't feeling well, then Ms. Martinez would say "Dexter, please don't . . . ," and then Dexter would throw up into the nearest trash can. Jacob thought Dexter's secret power was the most spectacular skill he had ever seen, and he finally had an opportunity to harness its limitless potential.

Jacob turned back toward Dexter, sneezed, and then nodded.

Dexter stood up and walked slowly toward Mr. Kruger's desk. He grabbed his stomach. "Mr. Kruger, I'm not feeling so well," he said.

Mr. Kruger held up his hands. "Dexter, stand back. Young man, please stand back!"

The mass sneezing was fading as the powder wore off. Jacob waited for Dexter to work his magic all over Mr. Kruger's desk.

Dexter froze in his tracks.

"Dexter?" Mr. Kruger pushed back his rolling chair into the corner. "What is wrong with you?"

"I think Dexter is sick, Mr. Kruger!" Jacob called out. "I think he's very, very sick!"

Just when they had reached the moment of truth, when the entire brilliant plan would come to its transcendent climax, Dexter instead hung his head and turned away from Mr. Kruger's desk. "It passed."

Jacob flushed with anger as the last sneezes rang out in the classroom. Another plan ruined by Dexter chickening out.

Suddenly the door to the classroom swung open and Jacob's old sixth-grade teacher Miss Banks walked

in. The last time he had seen her, he had been fleeing crazed substitute teachers on Planet Paisley. She had never returned to school, and while it was announced that she was taking a sabbatical, Jacob had a feeling it was because the route back to Earth was blocked by the space kapow.

Sarah gasped. "Miss Banks! You're back!"

Mr. Kruger held up his arms. "Miss Banks! You've chosen a most inopportune time to return. This classroom is a biological hazard!"

Miss Banks looked around at the children, who had stopped sneezing, and merely looked confused. "Um, thanks for the tip, Richard. I just need to speak to Jacob, Sarah, and Dexter please."

Mr. Kruger reached into his desk, pulled on a surgical mask, and eventually nodded.

Outside the classroom, the children hugged Miss Banks all at once. She looked exactly like they remembered her: short blond hair, glasses, and a wrinkled corduroy skirt.

"I can't believe you're back!" Sarah shouted.

Miss Banks flinched at Sarah's volume and looked around to see if anyone was watching. "Why yes, my personal leave was quite restorative and . . ." She was satisfied that no one was listening and leaned in. "Kids, they fixed the detour through the space kapow,

and space travel to Earth has resumed. Jacob, have you heard the news? I'm so proud of you! My own student!"

Jacob smiled, but then looked sheepishly over at Sarah. "Yeah . . . but I'm not running unless I have my campaign managers with me."

"Well, listen," Miss Banks said. "You must be careful. Things between space and Earth are worse than ever. The situation is . . . well, I fear it may be dangerous. We're counting on you children to make things right."

Jacob nodded. "We'll do our best."

"Good! I've arranged for the spaceship Lucy to meet you in the forest near your houses after dark."

"Lucy?" Dexter asked. "Couldn't we have at least gotten Praiseworthy? Lucy's so mean!"

Miss Banks smiled. "She told me to tell you that she was dreading seeing you children more than you could possibly imagine."

chapter 3

Jacob pulled the postcard out of his trash can and looked it over for the thousandth time. It was a painting of a cactus with snow-capped mountains in the background with the caption "Howdy y'all people, from Dakota, Arizona!" There was something off about the picture, and when Jacob had searched the Internet for "Dakota, Arizona," he couldn't find anything that matched. There was no such thing as a town called Dakota in Arizona.

He turned over the postcard and looked again at the inscription.

Dear Jacob,

Will pick you up for lunch at High Noon on April 23. Important things to discuss. I'm very proud of you. I love you.

Dad

HOWDY Y'ALL
PEOPLE, FROM
DAKOTA,
ARIZONA!

The stamp was for seven dollars, which Jacob would have thought was mysterious except that one of his memories of his dad was that he never seemed to know what anything cost.

He walked over to the shelf above his bed where he kept his grandfather's pipe, the one he had found in a junk shop on Planet Paisley. It was proof that his dad might be in outer space, that perhaps he was traveling around the universe losing heirlooms on strange planets. He set the postcard carefully alongside the pipe.

Jacob jumped when his cell phone beeped. He had a text from Sarah: *Outside, want 2 talk.*

He put on his shoes, yelled to his mom that he was going outside for a minute, and found Sarah sitting on the curb in front of his house. He sat down beside her,

and they stared at the forest down the street, where they both knew Lucy would arrive at any moment. The sun had set and the color was slowly draining from the sky. Jacob's breath caught when he thought of going back to space and seeing the impossible number of stars outside the window of a spaceship rocketing through the galaxy.

"What if you win?" Sarah asked quietly.

"Huh?"

Sarah turned and looked him in the eye. She brushed a strand of hair from her face. "What if you win, Jake? What then?"

He shrugged. "I haven't really thought through my whole campaign platform yet, but I had this great idea yesterday. Shouldn't it be a law that every restaurant should have either French fries or pizza on the menu? Or should it be both? I was thinking . . ."

Sarah put her hand on his arm and he stopped talking. "President of the universe. Think about how big that job is."

He jerked his arm back. "You don't think I can do it?"

She gently grabbed his arm again. "That's not what I'm saying. How are you going to do that job and still be a kid on Earth? You're going to have to be flying all over the place, solving problems and being responsible. What about our families? What about you and me? Dexter too," she added quickly. "I'll come with you for the election, but I can't just disappear into space forever, Jake. I can't do it."

Jacob nodded and was quiet for a moment. The idea of flying around space and never going to school didn't scare him at all, and he knew Miss Banks and the king were depending on him. He hoped there would be a way to convince Sarah and Dexter to stay with him in space instead of coming back and going to school every day and living their boring lives on Earth. If he had a choice between running around the universe or sitting through pre-algebra every day, he knew exactly which life he would choose.

He saw Dexter approaching, teetering with an overstuffed backpack that looked like it would tip him over at any moment. Suddenly the street lit up and there was a flash in the forest. A green laser shot up into the sky and then disappeared. A second later there was a faint whirring noise and a hiss. It was Lucy. Dexter gave Jacob and Sarah a hesitant thumbs-up.

Jacob thought about the postcard on his shelf, and the power he would have as president of the universe. He would be able to find anyone.

He turned to Sarah. "This is something I have to do."

chapter 4

Jacob turned away from the planets and stars whizzing by outside the cockpit and faced Sarah and Dexter instead. He held a yellow notepad and had a pen tucked behind his ear, some of the campaign supplies he had packed for the journey to Planet Headline.

"No more pranks," Jacob said. "No more tricks, no more practical jokes, no more breaking rules. That's all over. I have to show the people I'm responsible enough to run the entire universe."

Dexter tapped his cheek with his finger. "What about the sneezing powder this morning?"

"That was completely necessary!"

"How are we going to deal with your track record?" Sarah asked with a lopsided grin. "I think the news reporters are going to want to know about the time you lined your bedroom with plastic and tried to turn it into a giant hot tub."

Dexter high-fived Sarah. "That was hilarious! Oh, what about the time Jacob convinced the police department there was a grizzly bear trying to break *into* the zoo."

"Stop it!" Jacob shouted, and the edge in his voice made Sarah and Dexter look away. "This is serious."

"Excuse me, cretins," Lucy said, "I'd so hate to interrupt the future President Wonderbar's delusions of grandeur, but we are approaching the tunnel through the space kapow. While we're passing through, perhaps Mr. Wonderbar will want to figure out how he's going to expunge that catastrophe from the record as well."

Dexter and Sarah pursed their lips and Jacob could tell they were trying not to laugh.

"She's right," Jacob said. "We should probably come up with something."

"On it," Sarah said. She patted Jacob on the shoulder. "Don't worry."

He looked out the cockpit window and saw the tunnel, a shimmering tube that bore through the bright mess of stars and supernovas that had been left in the aftermath of the kapow. Lucy passed through slowly,

and it was almost as if they were on the inside of a kaleidoscope. The shifting colors shone brightly inside the cockpit, and Jacob was amazed the Astral engineers could have constructed something so vast and incredible in just a year.

He stared ahead at the small black dot of space at the end of the tunnel, but something irregular was blocking the view.

"Ugh." Lucy shuddered. "Children, we have trouble."

Jacob stood up and peered ahead as Lucy slowed down to a crawl. His eyes didn't want to believe what he was seeing, but as they drew closer, there was no mistake. It was a giant tree, with branches snaking up into the high reaches of the tunnel.

"What is a tree doing in the middle of the . . ." Jacob trailed off as he saw movement in the branches. "Are those . . . monkeys?!"

Six chimpanzees wearing clear space helmets were swinging around on the branches. An old metal spaceship was parked nearby.

"Space monkeys," Lucy said. "They always bring this infernal tree with them. I have to slow down to avoid these branches."

There was one large monkey hanging still at the

22

top of the tree, and Jacob could tell that it was staring at them.

"Are they intelligent?" Jacob asked.

"No, Jacob," Lucy said. "They are very, very stupid. That's why they're so dangerous."

"Where did they come from?" Sarah asked.

"They came from Earth. A Russian rocket accidentally blasted into space with test monkeys aboard and these are the descendents of those . . ." She trailed off. "This is not good."

Lucy drew closer and closer to the tree, which Jacob could now see was actually made of metal. Jacob locked eyes with the largest monkey. All of the other monkeys stopped what they were doing and stared at the spaceship.

Suddenly the big monkey bared his teeth and the other monkeys sprang into action. A few of them launched themselves at Lucy and began scrambling around on the outside of the ship, and others flew back toward their own ship. The big monkey leaped straight for the cockpit. Sarah shrieked when he landed with a thud. He pressed his helmet to the cockpit, his brown eyes looking over each of them.

"We're being boarded!" Lucy shouted.

Loud clangs rang throughout the hold, and on the

cockpit monitors Jacob could see that the monkeys were hitting the hull with metal rods.

"Children, they are causing serious damage!"

"Can you speed up?" Jacob asked.

They heard a loud crash, followed by screeching.

"They're inside!" Lucy shouted.

The big monkey scrambled off of the cockpit window.

"Lucy, do you have any weapons?" Jacob asked.

"I thought you said they were stupid!" Dexter yelled.

"They *are* stupid!" Lucy shouted. "They're even more hateful than you children."

One of the chimps scrambled up the staircase. He bared his teeth and jumped up and down, then ran up the wall and hung from the ceiling.

Soon the large chimp scrambled up as well. He had gray hair and seemed more intelligent than the others. He took off his helmet and paced in front of the children, looking at each of them in turn. He leaned close to Dexter, who leaned back in his chair in fright.

"Bad breath," Dexter whispered.

The monkey pushed Dexter in the chest and screeched. The monkey on the ceiling dropped down and grabbed Dexter, pulling him toward the staircase. They were joined by more monkeys, who swarmed

Dexter and stood between him and Sarah and Jacob.

"Ow!" Dexter yelped. "Guys, help me!"

"Leave him alone!" Sarah shouted.

Jacob jumped up, but the big monkey paced in front of him, blocking his way. The other monkeys pulled Dexter down the staircase and through the hold.

"Dexter!" Sarah yelled.

Jacob charged into the big monkey, who pushed him back roughly and slapped the ground. He bared his teeth and screeched, and then scrambled down the staircase. Jacob ran down the stairs after them, but he wasn't as fast as the monkeys. They had docked their spaceship alongside Lucy, and the big monkey had already made it back onto his ship. He turned back at Jacob and screeched in pleasure as the cargo door closed. There was a loud clang as the monkeys' ship disengaged.

Jacob ran back up the stairs and watched helplessly through the cockpit window as the tree folded back into the monkeys' spaceship and they blasted off, taking Dexter with them.

chapter 5

After them!" Sarah shouted.

Jacob watched the space monkey ship swerve erratically as it headed for the exit of the space kapow detour. He wasn't sure whether their swerving was a strategy to keep Lucy off the trail or whether the monkeys just weren't very good drivers.

"Children," Lucy said. "The monkeys have sent us a message."

"What do they want?!" Sarah asked.

"It's the word 'banana' repeated seven hundred times."

The end of the detour was looming, and when they exited Jacob knew the monkeys' ship could go in any direction. Lucy didn't have any nets or weapons, and there was no way to catch them. They would be forced to follow the monkey ship wherever it was going, and Jacob would surely miss the deadline to announce his candidacy.

"Do we have any bananas?" Sarah asked.

There was no way to get Dexter back that didn't involve giving in to the monkeys' demands. And Jacob knew that wasn't an option. "We can't," he said quietly.

"We can't what?" Sarah asked.

Jacob stared at the floor. "We can't give them what they want. I can't show weakness."

"Weakness?!" Sarah shrieked.

"We can't negotiate with space monkeys," Jacob said, seeing things with sudden clarity. He would soon be making decisions that would impact the entire universe, and it meant he had to think about more than just himself and his friends. "Word will get out in space that all you have to do to intimidate me is to kidnap my friends. I can't take that risk."

Sarah's jaw jutted out and her face flushed. She stood in front of Jacob and stared down at him. "Jacob Wonderbar," she said quietly. "Do you remember how you felt when you found out I had gone chasing after the diamond instead of rescuing you on Numonia? Do you remember how mad you were? Are you seriously telling me you are not going to go and rescue your best friend after he's been kidnapped by *space monkeys*?!"

Jacob turned his chair away and faced the control panel. "Lucy, please call Officers Bosendorfer and Erard."

"Fine," Lucy said.

"What are you doing?" Sarah asked.

After a few rings, someone picked up the intercom with a very loud and very long yawn. "Space officers," Officer Bosendorfer said finally. "I hope this isn't an emergency."

"Officer Bosendorfer, this is Jacob Wonderbar. I'd like to report a kidnapping. My friend Dexter has been taken by space monkeys, and . . ."

"Oh, this is ridiculous," Sarah said. "What are they going to do?"

"I agree with the girl," Officer Bosendorfer said. "What are we going to do? I hate space monkeys."

"Space monkeys?" Officer Erard said in the background. "Ugh. Tell them we're cracking a very important case."

"We're cracking a very important case," Officer Bosendorfer said. "It's terribly urgent. It's the Case of the Cracked . . . um, Case. Crime of the century."

Jacob's voice had an edge. "Are you space officers aware that I'm running for president of the universe?"

"Absolutely, Future President Wonderbar! I would vote for you twice if I could. Three times! It's just that these space monkeys are—"

"And are you aware that if I'm elected I will be able to pass laws about space officers and what happens to them when they refuse their responsibilities?"

"But—" Officer Bosendorfer said.

"And that I will be sure to remember which space officers were helpful to me before I was elected?"

There was a very long silence on the other end of the line. "Understood, Future President Wonderbar, Your, uh, Eminence. We will certainly find your friend."

"Good," Jacob said.

"And might I add," Officer Bosendorfer continued, "that your wisdom is a beautiful pearl that beacons in the stars of, um, space. May your reign be filled with the . . ."

Jacob switched off the intercom.

"They're not going to find him," Sarah said. "We have to do it ourselves."

Jacob stiffened in his chair. "I'm announcing my candidacy on Planet Headline in a few hours. That's my job, the space officers will do theirs, and if they don't, I'll replace them. I can't go chasing after space monkeys. Dexter will be okay."

Sarah slapped the wall. "I want no part of this. You hear me? None." She stormed down the stairs and Jacob heard the door to her stateroom slam shut.

Jacob stared out at the starry canopy of space. "Presidents have to make tough choices," he said to himself.

chapter 6

Dexter stared out of his cage at the young chimp that was watching his every move. When Dexter reached up to scratch his head the monkey scratched his head. When he paced inside his cage, the monkey paced in front of him. Finally Dexter crossed his eyes and the monkey stared at him for a moment before screeching and jumping around the room, flailing his arms, turning over some wooden crates, and making a horrible racket.

Dexter retreated to the back of the cage and sat down in the corner, feeling confident that he had broken a grave rule of monkey self-conduct.

When the monkeys had shoved him aboard their ship they placed him in a metal cage along with a bowl of water, some sunflower seeds, and a teddy bear. The bars were an inch thick, and although he had shoved against the door, it hadn't budged. He had no hope of escaping.

He tried to quell his racing heart and think rationally. He was sitting in a monkey cage on a monkey ship that was flying through space to who knows where. He would have been surprised at the turn of events, only he had been traveling on a ship piloted by Jacob Wonderbar. Of course he would be captured by space monkeys.

He buried his head in his hands and tried not to cry. The Era of Dexter, which had begun when he had helped rescue Jacob from deranged substitutes the first time they'd been in space, had already taken a severe blow when he had to dodge eighth-grade mutants during PE and sneak through back alleys whenever he walked home from school.

He had told himself that he would be brave in space, that he would finally put his scared ways behind him. And yet when the gray-haired chimp showed up in the cockpit he had wilted under pressure yet again. He froze and just went right along wherever the monkey pushed him.

Dexter lifted up his head and brushed off his shoulders. He was going to escape the cage. He was going to be brave.

"Hey," he shouted at the young chimp. "Let me out of here."

The chimp stared at him impassively.

Dexter walked over to the cage door and pantomimed turning a key and opening the lock. The monkey scrambled over and watched what he was doing.

After a moment the monkey screeched and ran over to the wall, where the key hung from a peg. He ran back over to Dexter and placed it on the floor.

Dexter lay down on the ground and reached as far as he could, but it was just a few inches out of reach. He stood up and frowned, and the chimp chirped happily.

He suspected the monkey was messing with him.

There was a commotion in the hall and the gray-haired monkey bounded in. He pointed at the door to Dexter's cage, and the young monkey opened it. The gray-haired monkey grabbed at Dexter's hand, but Dexter pulled back and retreated into the cage. He wasn't going anywhere with the monkey leader this time. The gray-haired monkey pounded the floor and scrambled into the cage. He grabbed Dexter's shoulder and pushed him out, and Dexter wasn't strong enough to resist.

The monkeys forced him down the hall and into the cockpit, which looked like something out of an old sci-

ence fiction movie. The dials and levers were old and rusted, and looked nothing like the futuristic screens aboard Lucy and Praiseworthy. The room was strewn with dried leaves and branches, and there were many dents in the walls and floor.

The gray-haired monkey pushed Dexter down into a chair and stared him in the eye for a moment. Dexter looked away, sensing that something important was about to happen.

The monkey leader scrambled over to a wall covered with small buttons. He pressed one, and a mechanical voice said, "Me." He pressed another and it said, "Boris."

He looked at Dexter to see if he understood. "Your name is Boris," Dexter said, realizing they actually had a way to communicate. He was beginning to think the monkeys were more intelligent than Lucy had given them credit for. "Where are you taking me, Boris?"

Boris pressed another button on the wall. The voice said, "Banana now." He held out his hand.

The monkeys began spinning in circles and screeching. One of the monkeys jumped up and grabbed a bar on the ceiling and swung himself around madly. The young monkey pounded the floor and bared his teeth.

Boris looked at Dexter, waiting with his hand out-

stretched. "I don't have any bananas," Dexter said.

Boris pressed the button. "Banana now."

"I don't have one."

Boris kept pressing the button with his hand outstretched. "Banana now. Banana now. Banana now. Banana now."

Dexter looked around at the monkeys, who were in a state of pandemonium. Two chimps got into a fight and began rolling around on the deck. Boris began jumping up and down and kept pressing the button.

"Banana now. Banana now. Banana now. Banana now. Banana now. Banana now. Banana now. Banana now . . ."

Dexter wished he were anywhere else in the entire universe.

chapter 7

What you don't know about running shoes may kill you, and tonight at ten, oxygen: Is it overrated? Find out the shocking truth in a special report that you *won't* want to miss."

Jacob couldn't figure out how the reporter had managed to make his hair so shiny. He wondered if he had undergone surgery to replace the entire top of his head with a permanently gleaming brow and rock-solid plastic hair.

Jacob looked around the room at the reporters, busily scratching at notepads and speaking into cameras. He was amazed at the many and varied places the reporters stowed their writing utensils. There were pens tucked behind ears, pens stuck into hair, pens tucked into stained shirts, and even two-fisted pens, with a second pen at the ready should one fail at the precise moment something important was spoken. There was paper all over the floor, and no one had thought to water any of the plants along the wall, which were brown and dead and themselves littered with more paper. Occasionally someone would shout, "Scoop! Scoop! I have a scoop!" and the other reporters would grumble to each other and then casually position themselves to eavesdrop on what the scooping reporter was saying.

"Are you getting this, you imbecile?!" the reporter screamed at his cameraman. "What? We're live? Ha-ha!" He adjusted his red tie. "Just a little joke for you folks back home."

Jacob looked all over the room for Sarah, and finally spotted her giving an interview in the back. He caught her eye, and though he knew she was still mad at him about Dexter, she gave him an encouraging smile.

"You're on," the reporter said. He glanced at his watch. "Is it time for more hair gel?" he asked his cameraman. "I think we need more gel."

Jacob steadied his nerves and stepped up to the podium, then onto the box behind the lectern. He peered out at the reporters, who were frantically taking pictures and scratching notes even though he hadn't said anything yet.

There were cameras everywhere, and he wondered how many billions of people were watching. Maybe even his dad was watching, either on some top-secret space TV channel on Earth, or maybe even from somewhere nearby in space. He pulled at the tie he was wearing, which Sarah had tied too tightly. He wondered if he should have spent more time on his speech.

"Astrals and Earthers," he began as confidently as he could. "I am supremely, uh, honored that you . . . I really appreciate that I'm here to be . . . I mean . . . I'm here to announce my candidacy for president of the universe."

Jacob waited for some sort of applause, but the reporters were staring at their notepads. After a moment, he finally heard clapping from the back and heard Sarah shout, "Go Jake!"

He cleared his throat. "This is an important time for Earth and Space. I mean, as I don't think I have to tell you. The first president of the universe should be like the king has been, um, like. Kind and good. And responsible. I promise to you that I will do the best job I can and will serve the office with honor."

He looked out at the reporters. Some of them had fallen asleep. The rest looked as if they were so bored they couldn't bother to keep their mouths closed. They

stared at Jacob with slack jaws and half-lidded eyes.

"Is that it?" someone finally asked.

"No," Jacob said quickly. "I mean, I will always do the right thing. I won't let you down. I promise. Uh, thank you."

One of the reporters threw his notepad into the air in disgust. "How can I write a story about this?" he shouted.

"Headline!" another yelled. "'Candidate for Presidency Promises to Try Hard.' Subhead: 'Reporter fired for boring everyone to death.'"

There was a murmur of agreement.

"How do you plan to beat your opponent?" someone asked.

Jacob frowned. "My opponent?" He hadn't even considered that he would have to run against anyone.

There was a commotion at the back of the room. Everyone turned and watched as an entourage swooped in with a great deal of fanfare. Cameras flashed, and the reporters started shouting questions. Through the tumult, Jacob finally caught a glimpse of his opponent—a small figure with impeccably groomed hair standing in the center of his entourage. It was Mick Cracken. Space buccaneer and prince.

Mick guided the entourage to the aisle, then broke away. He walked confidently up to the podium and

shoved Jacob aside, then stood in front of the microphone. Jacob gave his ground, too stunned to know how to react.

Mick flashed his best cocky smile. "To the finest reporters and journalists in the universe, guardians of free speech and keepers of liberty. I bow down before your beauty and intelligence, you peerless scribes of truth and wisdom."

The reporters nodded to each other and smiled. There was a smattering of applause. Jacob didn't know what to do and locked eyes with Sarah Daisy, who shook her head and shrugged.

Mick paused for a moment, basking in the glow of attention. Finally he began to speak. "My administration will be full of corruption and scandal. There will be foul tricks and dirty deeds. I will disgrace the office, and my mistakes will force me to beg for mercy." Mick looked up at the reporters. "There will probably be tears."

The reporters murmured to each other appreciatively.

"As the universe's most famous space buccaneer, I couldn't be more unqualified for this office. I cannot promise you that I will be competent or wise or good or even sort of good. You will often wonder how and why you elected me in the first place. That is, if I don't

steal votes outright." Mick winked, and the reporters laughed. "There will always be a scandal to follow. Always a conspiracy to unravel. Constant speculation about whether I will be forced to resign.

"Above all else, you will never be bored. I will break every single promise I make to you, except for this one, which I will hold dear: My speeches will be short."

The room grew quiet in excitement and anticipation.

"And that is why it gives me great pleasure to announce my candidacy for president of the universe."

The reporters rose to their feet and cheered wildly. Mick raised his hands above his head and shook them in triumph.

Mick walked over to Jacob and turned him to face the crowd. "Photo op," he said. He grabbed Jacob's

hand to shake it and flashed a peace sign with his left hand, giving the reporters his biggest smile.

"This is going to be so easy," Mick said between his teeth.

Jacob sensed that his candidacy was on thin ice.

chapter 8

Jacob was still stunned long after Mick's speech had sent the reporters into a frenzy. He watched Mick work the room, laughing at reporters' jokes and reminiscing with them about how terrible he had been to them when he was a toddler running around Planet Royale. Every now and then he would turn to wink at Jacob, clearly relishing that he had so thoroughly upstaged his opponent.

Not knowing quite what to do, Jacob found a video screen to stare at and was surprised to see his old friend Moonman from the tiny planet Numonia. He was being interviewed in front of the spaceship Swift and looked as if he was the only person in the universe more uncomfortable than Jacob.

"Why . . . Jacob Wonderbar? Of course I remember him," he said.

A reporter stuck his microphone closer to Moon-man's face and he flinched. "Could you please comment on reports that the Earther candidate is here to bring war to Astral colonies and is advancing a hard-line pro-Earth agenda?"

Moonman screwed up his face and regained some composure. "Now you listen here," he said. "You couldn't find a finer young man than Jacob Wonderbar and we would be lucky to have such a . . . a . . . fine young man for president. He's welcome back on Numonia anytime, which is more than I could say for all of you rotten . . ."

Night fell on Numonia at that moment and Moon-man fell asleep standing up.

"Sir?" the reporter asked, alarmed. "Sir!"

"Well, well, well . . ." Jacob heard a girl say behind him.

Jacob turned around and saw Catalina Penelope Cassandra Crackenarium, princess of the universe, dressed in a smart pantsuit and wearing sensible pearl earrings. Her brown hair was pulled back into a bun.

"Wow, Cat . . . Hi. I'm . . ."

Sarah suddenly appeared at Jacob's elbow. "What are *you* doing here?"

"Sarah Daisy!" Catalina shouted. She grabbed Sarah in a tight hug, air-kissed her cheeks, then held her by the shoulders. "Now let's get a look at you." She looked Sarah's outfit up and down, raised her eyebrows, and then shrugged. "Enh," she said.

Sarah's face flushed and Jacob stepped in between them in case Sarah was considering an attack. "It's good to see you, Cat. Are you here because of Mick?"

Catalina laughed merrily and tapped him on the nose. "Don't be silly! I'm here because of you, sweetie." She spread her arms. "I'm going to be your running mate."

Sarah sputtered. "You! Don't be ridiculous."

"And your vice president when you win."

"That's really nice," Jacob said. "But I think we're doing fine with what we—"

"Jake . . ." Catalina said. "Oh, Jake, honey. That"— she pointed to the podium where Jacob had delivered his speech—"was not fine. You two don't know the first thing about Astrals or how you can win."

"We know enough," Sarah said.

"Oh really?" Cat said. "What are you doing for communications? Do you have Astral Tellys so you can make calls to the press? Let alone keep up with Astral television stations?"

Sarah and Jacob looked at each other.

Catalina laughed. "Did you think your pitiful Earther phones were going to work in outer space?"

"No," Jacob said. "But . . ."

"Population centers. Sarah darling, why don't you share with Candidate Wonderbar the five most populous planets and how you plan to campaign there for votes? What about the three Battles Supreme? Have you thought about your strategy? We have less than a starweek to prepare for the first one."

Sarah was silent. Jacob hadn't heard anything about any battles.

Catalina grabbed Jacob's tie and flipped it dismissively. "And look how you have my future husband dressed. The poor dear!"

Jacob looked down at his red tie. He didn't think it was so bad.

"You need credibility. You need Astrals to trust you. And what better way than with the Astral princess as your running mate?"

"What's in it for you?" Sarah finally managed to say.

"Me?" Catalina looked scandalized. "Why, I couldn't be thinking less about myself at a time like this. I just want to help Jake win this election."

"Right. Sure. Like I'd listen to a stupid *alien,*" Sarah whispered furiously. Catalina's eyes widened in shock.

She started to say something back, but then stopped.

Sarah grabbed Jacob's arm. "Let's go."

"Sarah, look . . ."

Sarah paused and stared daggers at him. "Jacob Wonderbar, if you go along with this . . ."

Jacob wasn't sure he had ever seen Sarah quite as angry, but he also knew that Catalina was right. He didn't know how to run this election and he did need someone like her to give him credibility with the Astrals. It was the only chance he had at rescuing his candidacy, especially after the terrible speech he had given.

"We have to," he said.

Sarah pushed Jacob's arm away and stomped off. "I'm taking Lucy and I'm going to find Dexter," she shouted over her shoulder.

The reporters sensed a conflict and swooped in, camera bulbs flashing, video cameras rolling. "Mr. Wonderbar! Mr. Wonderbar! Would you care to comment on your friend Sarah Daisy leaving your campaign? Mr. Wonderbar!"

"Um . . ." he started.

Catalina stepped confidently in front of the cameras. "Jacob Wonderbar has decided that he needed to shake up his staff in order to energize his campaign.

Sarah Daisy has resigned her position and acknowledged her abysmal performance as chief of staff."

Jacob frowned. He started to defend Sarah, but Catalina continued, "The campaign will be heading in a new direction. Mr. Wonderbar has offered me the opportunity to be his running mate." She flashed Jacob a dazzling smile. "And I couldn't be happier to take it."

chapter 9

After two hours spent pressing the "Banana now" button, the space monkeys had eventually grown tired of their antics and fallen asleep in a heap in the cockpit. Dexter thought about trying to determine where the spaceship was heading, but he was so tired and so grateful that the monkeys were finally quiet that he huddled in a corner and wrapped his arms around his knees. He put his head down and began to nod off.

The young chimp that had been watching Dexter when he was in the cage scrambled over to him. He chirped quietly and then rested his head on Dexter's shoulder.

Dexter didn't have the heart to move away from him, though he was thoroughly terrified at the thought that the monkeys had begun to think he was one of them.

"What's your name?" he asked the monkey.

The monkey didn't answer, but Dexter decided to call him Rufus until he could get him to press the buttons on the wall. Dexter yawned and was feeling very drowsy . . .

Dexter heard a crash and realized he had fallen asleep. The monkeys all leaped up at once and began swinging around the cockpit, crashing into things and screeching and causing a horrible racket.

As he began to regain his senses, Dexter realized they weren't flying through space anymore. He looked out the cockpit window and saw what looked like a giant airplane hangar. They had landed on another planet.

He heard another crash in the hold, and the monkeys scrambled around, clearly terrified. They backed into a corner, and Boris paced in front of them.

Suddenly men wearing army uniforms and body armor scrambled into the cockpit. They were carrying blasters, and as they drew closer Dexter could see that they had an unbelievable number of knives and weapons hanging from their belts. Dexter's heart leaped. He was finally being rescued.

The men charged in, diving and rolling on the

ground, leaping up, and shouting things like "Cover me!" and "Move! Move! Move!" They looked like hyperactive martial arts experts with guns. Dexter wasn't sure why the men needed to employ such complex maneuvers to board an unarmed spaceship, but they seemed to be enjoying themselves.

Boris charged at one of the soldiers and they knocked him back with a stick. Dexter suddenly became worried for Boris's safety. "Boris, don't!" he shouted.

The monkeys all ran at once out of the cockpit, and the soldiers followed them with their guns at the ready. Dexter scrambled after them and reached the hold just in time to see the monkeys being herded safely into a nearby bunker. Dexter was relieved that they hadn't been hurt. He was even more relieved that he was finally free of them.

"Thank you!" he shouted to the soldiers. "You don't know how long I've been . . ."

"Freeze!" one of the soldiers shouted at him, swinging his blaster around. Dexter raised his hands.

"It's fine, I'm—"

"Silence!" the soldier shouted.

After a tense moment, a beefy kid with bright yellow hair stepped into the hold. He looked like he was about Dexter's age, and he wore the same uniform as the soldiers, though he had far more decorative rib-

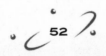

bons and medals. His nose was very crooked and it gave his face the appearance of being locked in a perpetual sneer.

"Good work, men," the boy said. He paced in front of Dexter for a little while. Then he stepped up and sniffed at him. "So, what's it like being a dirty Earther?"

Dexter blinked in confusion. He didn't like the way this rescue was unfolding. "Um. Well, I don't know, I never really thought of it like that, I guess I don't . . ."

The boy punched Dexter hard on the shoulder.

"Ow! What was that for?" Dexter yelped.

"My dad said to punch first and ask questions later."

Dexter rubbed his shoulder. "But you asked me a question first and then punched me. You didn't even have the order right!!"

The boy grunted. Dexter didn't have the sense that he was very bright.

"Splendid operation, men!" Dexter heard a voice outside say. He turned and looked as an adult version of the yellow-haired boy strode into the hold. His uniform could barely contain the ribbons, medals, and badges that poked out from every available space on his uniform.

"Did you punch him, Patrick?" the man asked.

Patrick shot Dexter an evil smile. "I sure did."

"That's my boy," the man said. He loomed over Dexter. "General Gravy is the name, and you're coming with me."

"This wasn't a rescue, was it?" Dexter said, sighing.

"A rescue?" General Gravy said. "Dear bombs no, this was a training exercise. I wanted my men to have experience rescuing high-value targets and . . ." He looked closer at Dexter. "You're not Jacob Wonderbar."

Dexter stared in shock for a moment before he was able to say, "Why would I be Jacob Wonderbar?"

"I told them to get Jacob Wonderbar!" General Gravy shouted. He threw his hat to the ground, and Patrick shrunk back.

General Gravy's face was red as he stomped away. "Never send a monkey to do a man's job," he muttered. He turned back before he exited the ship and shouted, "Lock this Earther up!"

Patrick gave Dexter a gleeful poke and led him off the ship. The soldiers marched him into the giant bunker and down an industrial hallway with metal floors, lit with circular headlamps with bulbs that flickered occasionally.

Patrick pushed open a door that led to a room full of monkey cages. Dexter's throat caught when he saw the space monkeys all locked up, shrieking and banging on the walls.

One of the soldiers unlocked the door to one of the cages and pointed. "In you go."

Dexter's heart sank. "Not again."

The soldiers pushed him in, and Dexter found himself once again in a monkey cage, this time with the little chimp who had befriended him on the ship. Rufus crawled into his arms and gave him a hug. He was much heavier than Dexter expected, and he struggled to take a breath.

He patted the monkey on the back. "I guess we're in this together."

chapter 10

Just when Sarah thought she had dodged the last of the reporters, a small camera shot up through a grate on the sidewalk and flashed in her face.

"Leave me alone!" she shouted.

The reporters had thought of everything. They'd followed her into the bathroom at the press center, out onto the street, and continued shouting questions at her no matter how many times she said "No comment." Finally she had just started running and eventually outlasted the reporters, but she knew they could be lurking around every corner.

She heard a vehicle approaching. She ducked into a doorway and hid her face as a flying news van with satellites on the roof sped by.

The whole thing was ridiculous and she just wanted to go home. Jacob had already been hypnotized by the stupid princess of the universe and wouldn't even try to rescue his best friend, never mind that *he* had been a quivering wreck when Sarah had left him behind on Numonia once upon a time. And to think her biggest worry had been that he would forget all about her when he was busy passing laws and flying around the universe. No, he was already betraying her and Dexter just a few hours into the election. She hoped he'd lose in a landslide.

As she stepped back onto the sidewalk, a manhole cover flew off and clanged down the street. The reporters started climbing out of it, looking very pleased with themselves.

"You were in the sewers?!"

They were covered in grime and smelled terrible, but were soon pressing microphones in front of her and shouting questions.

She was quickly surrounded by the pack and couldn't move.

"Miss Daisy! Miss Daisy!"

One of the young reporters elbowed a cameraman in the face and then jostled her way to the front. "Miss Daisy!" she shouted. "Is it true that Jacob Wonderbar is the most wanted criminal on Earth?"

Sarah smirked and almost shouted "Yes," as well as many other lies that could sink his campaign, but she was too hurt by Jacob's decision to even summon insults. She looked at the ground for a moment, and said, "Jacob Wonderbar? I don't even really know him anymore. Now, if you'll excuse me . . ."

She started to walk forward, but the reporters weren't satisfied and started shouting more questions. Sarah clenched her fists.

"Oh wow!" she yelled. "I heard there's a kitten being rescued from a tree by a very cute fireman only a few blocks from here! What an uplifting story, you'd better hurry!"

The reporters looked at one another for a moment and then all started running away, pushing and shoving each other as they scrambled off in different directions. Sarah was finally free.

She made her way back to the spaceship parking facility, where Lucy was waiting. If Jacob was too occupied to go rescue Dexter Goldstein, she'd just have to do it herself. She was just about to board when a figure stepped out from the shadows.

"Going somewhere, Sarah Daisy?"

Mick Cracken grinned at her.

"Ugh. What do you want?" Sarah asked.

Mick's teeth looked whiter than ever, and Sarah

wasn't sure she had ever seen hair parted in a straighter, more perfect line, which was really saying something, considering some of the hairstyles she had seen on some of the reporters.

"I don't think your talents were properly utilized by the Wonderbar campaign," he said. "What a disappointment that you were forced out under such . . . dubious circumstances."

"Right. Sure. Nice of you to worry about my feelings, Mick. Good seeing you and everything, but I'm . . . yeah." Sarah stepped toward Lucy.

"I want you to be my running mate."

Sarah stopped in her tracks and turned back to face him. "What?"

Mick looked incredibly pleased that he had her interest. "I want you to be my running mate. I could use you in the campaign."

Sarah looked around the parking facility. "Is this one of your stupid tricks? Are there cameras somewhere recording this?"

Mick acted like he was in a great deal of pain. "Oh Sarah, surely you think more of me than that."

"Nope."

Mick smiled.

"This isn't a trick," he said. "I have the reporters on

standby for a press conference. We could announce it immediately."

Sarah tried to figure out why Mick would want her on the campaign. While she hated to even consider the idea that anything Princess Pointyhead said remotely resembled the truth, Catalina was definitely right that Sarah really didn't know much about Astrals and how to run an interplanetary presidential campaign. And it was becoming abundantly clear that most Astrals thought Earthers were dangerous. So what could Sarah possibly offer Mick that would help him in a campaign?

She imagined standing beside Mick at a press conference, announcing that she was his running mate, and it suddenly dawned on her.

"It would look bad for Jacob if one of his friends decided to run against him."

Mick feigned confusion. "Would it really? Oh. Why . . . I hadn't thought of that, I was just hoping to have your talents to help me . . ."

"Spare me," Sarah said.

She knew Jacob would be furious if he found out that Sarah was campaigning against him, but he had already dumped her overboard for Princess Pointyhead, so it wasn't as if his hands were so clean. And if she was helping Mick's campaign, she could make sure that Jacob would really lose, and once Mick won she could resign the vice presidency and go back to Earth with Jacob after the election. Then everything would finally go back to normal.

Plus, she thought, gaining a little bit of steam and confidence, Mick was right about one thing. Her talents really weren't utilized in the Wonderbar campaign. Astral knowledge or not, it wasn't as if she was completely useless.

"I'll think about it," she said.

Mick nodded as if he expected this. "Would you at least like a tour of my new ship?"

She walked with him over to a sparkling black spaceship. It was long and sleek, forming a perfect triangle with a small teardrop of a cockpit on top. There were two massive boosters at the back, and a small gangway leading into the hold. The words "Mick Jr." were plated in silver cursive along the side.

"What's this?" she asked.

"This," Mick said, his voice bursting with pride, "is my new spaceship. I had a hand in designing every detail. It's the fastest ship in the universe, the most luxurious . . . it has stealth capabilities and the greatest gaming system on any spaceship in the universe."

He ran his fingers lovingly along the hull, then

took out a handkerchief and carefully wiped the place where he had touched it.

"Where did you get this?"

"It was my twelfth birthday present," he said.

Sarah recalled Mick's father, the king of the universe, saying that Mick was done flying spaceships for a while. "How did you convince your dad to give you this?"

Mick looked terribly concerned about a tiny speck that had appeared on the hull. He gave it a gentle flick and then sighed in relief. "Um. It might have also been a reward for finally getting a D in Earther Studies."

"Wow, Mick. Your dad must be so proud."

Mick didn't seem to notice her sarcasm, and when he reached the gangway, he bowed and gestured. "After you, mademoiselle."

He led her onto the ship, which was all gleaming black plastic and leather inside. Electronic lounge music was playing softly. There was a large painting on one of the walls, upon which was spray-painted "Mick Rules!" Sarah noted that the painting was signed by Mick Cracken.

"So?" Mick asked. "What do you think?"

Sarah thought about the election ahead, and she knew she had to do it. She wanted to make sure Jacob would lose, even if that meant aligning herself with a

conceited buccaneer with poor taste in art.

"All right, Mick," Sarah sighed. "Fine. I'll do it. But on one condition. Dexter Goldstein was captured by space monkeys, and we have to find him, or I quit."

Mick's eyes glinted, but he didn't smile. "I think that can be arranged."

Sarah crossed her arms. "Last time we made a deal you were lying out of your teeth."

"I'm sure that won't happen again," Mick said.

She didn't believe him, but she didn't see much of a choice either. It wasn't as if she knew how to save Dexter from space monkeys. She waited a moment before saying, "Fine." She reached out and shook, then had a sudden urge to disinfect her hands.

"See, Mick Jr.?" Mick shouted. "I told you she'd agree!"

"Ha!" Mick's voice echoed back. "Great work, master. The presidency will soon be ours . . . Er . . . I mean yours . . ."

Sarah's jaw dropped. "You programmed the ship's nav system to be . . . you? The spaceship talks like you?!"

Mick looked immensely pleased with himself.

Sarah was already beginning to regret her decision.

chapter 11

Jacob almost didn't recognize the space-ship Praiseworthy. He was painted a brilliant orange and decorated with impressive metallic streamers. The dainty horses carved into the exterior had blazing golden manes, and the lace and frill were adorned to look like flags. The last time Jacob had seen Praiseworthy, the ship had been painted a sloppy black by Mick Cracken, and Praiseworthy himself had been thrilled with the color scheme, feeling it gave him a more threatening image as a buccaneer ship.

"Master Wonderbar," Praiseworthy exclaimed when Jacob stepped on board. "I couldn't be more pleased! Welcome!"

"They painted you orange? What about your days as a buccaneer vessel?"

"Oh, Master Wonderbar, your memory is quite impressive. I did enjoy my days as a dashing buccaneer ship, but I couldn't be happier with my new color. When Princess Catalina told me I might be the personal escort vessel for the future president of the universe, I swiftly asked the maintenance crews to paint me orange. It *is* your favorite color, isn't it, Master Wonderbar?"

Jacob smiled as he sat down in the copilot seat. "Thanks, Praiseworthy."

Catalina tossed a small gadget into Jacob's lap. It was a piece of plastic, orange on one side and black on the other. "Your Astral Telly," she said. Jacob noticed that she held on to her own, which was purple and encrusted with jewels. "You're going to love this. You don't even have to turn a hand crank for a half hour like you do with your pathetic Earther phones."

"Um. We don't—"

"Quick demonstration. Just say 'Call' and the name of the person you want to talk to and let the Telly do the rest. When you want to hang up, just say 'End call.' Like so . . ."

Catalina held up her phone and said, "Call Michaelus Cracken." She waited a moment, and Mick's face appeared on Catalina's screen.

He scowled and said, "What?"

"You're ugly. End call." Mick's face dissolved to black. Catalina smiled brilliantly at Jacob. "See how that works?"

"Okay . . ."

"You can use it to watch television too. Just say the station you want to watch. You'll probably want to watch a lot of ANN, so be sure and—"

"What's A-N-N?"

Catalina froze, and then took a deep breath as if to steady herself. "Oh my. Jacob Wonderbar, you have so much to learn. ANN. It stands for Astral News Network. They're going to be covering the election twenty-five zoomecs a starweek."

Jacob looked down at his phone and said, "ANN."

Sarah Daisy appeared on his screen, and with a flash Jacob found himself inside a spaceship watching Sarah. She was standing in front of a microphone next to Mick Cracken in what looked like a trendy nightclub, or at least the décor was entirely black and there was soft lounge music playing. He turned and looked around and no one seemed to have noticed his arrival. Jacob waved at Sarah, but she didn't see him. Everywhere he looked, the ANN logo was etched into the corner of his vision.

She seemed to be giving a speech, and she was saying, ". . . and that is why I've decided to become Mick Cracken's running mate."

"No!" Jacob shouted, but no one heard him.

"Why do you think Mick Cracken will make a good president?" a reporter asked.

There had to have been a mistake. Sarah said she was finding Dexter and going back to Earth. He couldn't begin to understand why she was campaigning for president with his worst enemy.

Sarah stared straight ahead. "He's . . . Um . . . Well, he's . . . Wow. The question is, why do I think Mick Cracken will make a good president?" She looked over at a beaming Mick Cracken. Sarah stalled for a few moments longer, staring at Mick, before she finally nodded to herself and said, "He doesn't always smell."

Jacob felt completely numb. "How do I get out of here? I want out of here!" he yelled.

From somewhere outside his head Catalina said, "Just say 'Off.'"

"Off. Now." Jacob said, but it didn't work.

"Not 'Off now,' just 'Off.'"

He yelled, "Off!" and he found himself back aboard Praiseworthy. He threw the Telly into Catalina's hands.

"What is that thing? How was I inside that ship?"

Catalina looked at Jacob as if he had gone insane. "Um. It's called television."

Jacob tried to make sense of Sarah joining Mick's campaign. He knew that she was upset that he hadn't immediately gone to rescue Dexter, and of course she wasn't happy when he agreed to let Catalina join the campaign, but he never thought she'd try and get back at him by siding with his worst enemy. He thought back to their last trip to space and the way Sarah and Mick had seemed oddly close after spending so much time together trying to steal the Dragon's Eye . . .

Maybe Mick had been the whole reason she wanted to get back to space in the first place. She could have been lying when she said she was going to look for Dexter. It all could have just been an excuse so she could go run off with Mick.

"Hey," Catalina said.

She took Jacob's hands and made him sit up.

"Don't worry about a thing. You still have the prettier running mate!" She reached out to hug him.

Jacob frowned, knowing how offended Sarah would be if she heard Catalina say that.

"You know they have a crush on each other," Catalina said softly.

Jacob's mood darkened further.

"Hey, hey," Catalina said gently. "I'm here for you,

Jakey. *I* know how great you are, and she's just crazy if she's too blind to see it."

"Thanks," Jacob mumbled as he accepted Catalina's hug. His brain felt like it was spinning in circles, and he was at least glad to have someone there with him who thought he was great, someone who was famous and a princess and who happened to be correct when she bragged about being pretty.

"I know just the thing to distract you," Catalina said.

"What?"

"Praiseworthy, please set your course for Planet Dork."

"What's Planet Dork?" Jacob asked.

Catalina smiled. "I think you may know it as Planet Archimedes."

Jacob stood up quickly and said, "No way." He definitely knew that planet. The last time he had been there he had been captured by insane scientists and deported to a planet full of substitute teachers. "Why are we going there?"

"Because you need a history lesson."

Jacob's Telly buzzed to life. Catalina stared at it for a moment and then tossed it over to him.

"Looks like the press knows you're registered. You have seven hundred missed calls."

chapter 12

"All right, out you go! Bananas for everyone!" Patrick Gravy opened the cage doors and the monkeys scrambled out. "Not that you deserve them, filthy monsters . . ."

Rufus tugged on Dexter's hand, but he resisted and stayed in the cage.

"Earthers too," Patrick said, stepping over to Dexter's cage with a happy sneer. He was clutching a small bat, which he tapped on the edge of the cage. "Don't make me get nasty."

Dexter wondered what Patrick's nasty side could possibly look like, considering how rotten his good side had been, but he decided not to test him to find out. He stepped out of the cage, his body sore from the cramped quarters and from holding Rufus. He had trouble sleeping the night before. Not only were the quarters tiny and dank, but every few minutes a muffled bang outside shook his cage and woke him up.

He had spent some time trying to figure out how he had possibly ended up held captive in a cage by strange soldiers, but he could not begin to make sense of it. He wondered if Sarah and Jacob were trying to rescue him or if they even knew where he was. But there was really only one conclusion to be reached: He had to escape.

Patrick and a heavily armed soldier marched the monkeys out of the bunker and into a small forest, which was surrounded by a high fence covered with several different types of barbed wire. Dexter saw some sparks emitting from the fence and figured it must be electrified. The planet's sun was shining very brightly and intensely, and the trees looked like pine trees on Earth, though they had broad orange leaves. Dexter saw a flash out of the corner of his eye and then barely ducked in time as a huge buzzing insect the size of a small bird nearly collided with his head. It looked like an overgrown dragonfly, and Dexter could have sworn it licked its insect lips as it passed.

"What was that?!" he shouted.

"Knifefly," Patrick said. "Watch out for those, they'll make you bleed for sure." He sounded quite

pleased by the idea. "'Course, we officers have knife-fly repellant."

"Where are we?" Dexter asked.

Patrick laughed, which Dexter thought sounded like a taxicab honking. He elbowed a soldier next to him. "Get a load of this, Madrigal. Dirty Earther doesn't know where we are."

"Pathetic, sir," Madrigal said.

"I'd like to get back to my friends," Dexter said quietly. "Isn't this kidnapping? Isn't it against the law? I mean, I met the king and he didn't seem like the type to—"

Patrick stuck a stubby finger into Dexter's chest. "The king's just about finished, Earther, and he's not going to protect your stupid planet anymore. You'd do well to avoid mentioning his name around here, because as soon as he's elected, Mick Cracken is going to—"

Madrigal cleared his throat, and said, "Sir . . . Your father said not to mention . . ."

"Yeah, yeah." Patrick waved Madrigal away and pressed his lips together, his face turning redder than it already was. He pushed Dexter toward the forest. "Time for your bananas."

Dexter decided he'd rather spend time with space monkeys than with Patrick Gravy and walked through

the gate in the direction of the racket the chimps were making. He could see them in the distance, swinging around in the trees and eating bananas. Patrick slammed the gate behind him.

Dexter was completely unsurprised to hear Patrick say the name Mick Cracken. He had already suspected that Mick was somehow behind the entire ordeal. Kidnapping Dexter with space monkeys probably wasn't even the most nefarious thing Mick Cracken had done that day. But even though Dexter had a strong feeling that Mick was behind it, it didn't help the more pressing matter of how Dexter was going to . . .

"Psst . . ."

Dexter heard a noise from the bushes, and he looked around for a stick in case one of Patrick's goons was about to attack him.

"Pssssst . . ." he heard again. He saw big figures hiding in the bush, and he thought they looked quite familiar.

"It's Officers Bosendorfer and Erard," Officer Bosendorfer whispered loudly. "We're here to rescue you."

"And hurry up, because we're tired of eating bananas," Officer Erard added.

Dexter crept over to the bush, and he could see that Officers Bosendorfer and Erard were dressed in cam-

74

ouflage and had even taped foliage to their helmets. They clearly had thought they would blend in, but their pink skin gave them away. Their large bodies were heaving in the heat, and there was a massive pile of banana peels nearby.

"Right," Officer Erard said. "Now then. Let's get out of here. We're under strict orders to return you to Candidate Wonderbar."

"You talked to Jacob? Where is he?"

"I say," Officer Bosendorfer said, looking at his watch. "It's almost time for their blasted—"

Dexter was thrown to the ground by a shockwave and deafened by the sound of a massive explosion. The monkeys screeched nervously in the trees, and Dexter saw a fireball rise from the field nearby. He heard hearty cheering, and Patrick's distinctive high voice yelling, "That one was awesome!"

"What was that?!" Dexter asked.

"Morning missile," Officer Bosendorfer said. "They don't like to go more than a few parcelticks without setting one off. They're a bunch of crazy goons, and if I had my way we'd lock up the whole lot of them on Planet Clink."

Dexter stood up carefully. Between knifeflies, missile explosions, and surly kid soldiers, he wasn't sure what he should fear the most. He was terrifically

relieved that the officers had come to rescue him, even if he felt a stab of disappointment that Jacob and Sarah hadn't come with them.

The officers turned and walked toward their police cruiser, which was hovering a short distance away, covered with twigs and sticks.

Dexter turned back and saw Rufus rolling through some leaves, throwing a banana up and down to himself and having a great time, and his heart sank. If he left Rufus behind, he knew the monkeys would be locked back up in a cage and forced to go kidnap whoever Patrick's crew decided needed kidnapping that day. He didn't know the space monkeys very well, but it didn't seem like a very noble life, and they didn't seem to like Patrick and General Gravy very much.

"Hang on," he called out to the officers. "We have to take the monkeys."

"Allergic," Officer Bosendorfer said quickly. "Terrible allergy. Can't think when I'm around them. I go blind."

"My mother was killed by a rogue band of space monkeys," Officer Erard said. "I have never forgiven them."

Officer Bosendorfer covered his mouth in panic. "Your mother is dead? When did this happen?! She sent me a lovely Astralday card just last week and . . ."

Officer Erard gave him a stern nudge, and Officer Bosendorfer's eyes widened in understanding. He turned to Dexter and said, "It was an unspeakable tragedy. Such a wonderful woman."

Dexter heard a distant "tweep" followed by a loud crack nearby. A small fire and some smoke rose out of the tree next to him.

"Intruders!" he heard Patrick shout. Dexter turned just in time to see Patrick take a shot at him with his blaster.

Dexter dove behind a tree nearby. Officers Bosendorfer and Erard gave each other a nod and then scrambled for their ship. He saw Boris up in the branches nearby, hissing at Patrick and Madrigal.

"Boris!" he shouted. "Millions and millions of bananas."

Boris stared intently at Dexter and he knew he had his attention. He pointed at the officers' space cruiser. "Banana now! Banana now!"

Boris screeched, and the monkeys started scrambling for the space cruiser. Dexter followed behind them, looking over his shoulder in time to see Patrick readying another shot. Dexter dove to the ground and heard a crack where his head had just been. He scrambled on board.

"Let's get out of here!"

He ran up to the cockpit. Officer Bosendorfer was trying to take off while Rufus sat happily on his shoulders.

Officer Erard stared at a piece of plastic, and muttered, "Pick up . . . pick up . . ." He shook his head and set it down. "Jacob Wonderbar has his Telly turned off, and the spaceship Lucy says he's not on board and good riddance."

"Where should we take these beasts?" Officer Bosendorfer said. He was frantically checking monitors.

Dexter felt a shove from behind. He turned around to see Boris, with his hand outstretched. They didn't have translation software aboard, but Dexter was certain what the voice would have said. "Banana now."

Dexter tried to think about where he could go to quickly get the monkeys some bananas before they completely destroyed the inside of the cruiser. It would take too long to get back through the space kapow detour, and he knew there were no bananas on Numonia or Planet Archimedes, so that left . . . Dexter smiled. He knew exactly where they should go.

"Planet Royale."

chapter 13

After his phone rang incessantly during their one-zoomec, or eight Earth hours, flight to Planet Archimedes, Catalina finally taught Jacob how to program the Astral Telly so that it would only ring when people he really wanted to speak to were calling. He immediately added Dexter, as well as the king and Miss Banks, and after a great deal of thought he decided to add Mick Cracken and Sarah Daisy as well.

His heart raced when he thought about adding one more person, someone he had wanted to talk to for years, but he wondered if he was being foolish. He checked to make sure that Catalina wasn't looking, and then he quickly whispered his dad's name to the list of approved callers. He stared at the Telly for a moment and thought about trying to call his dad to see if he was somewhere out in space. All he had to do was say "Call Dad," but he couldn't bring himself to do it, and an indignant feeling stirred within him instead. He was running for president. His dad would know he was in space. After not showing up or calling for years, his dad should have been the one to call and apologize.

"Are you ready?" Catalina asked.

Jacob nodded, and they stepped out onto the street on Planet Archimedes. He saw the familiar sight of scientists walking up and down the sidewalks, staring into the sky and bumping into each other since they weren't watching where they were going. Nearly everyone was wearing the automatically focusing binoculars that Jacob had seen a guard wearing on his last trip. Apparently the guard had started a fad.

Even though they were entering the Astral History Museum during normal hours and hadn't done anything wrong, Jacob watched the scientists warily, ready for one of them to leap out and arrest him like last time.

"Watch out!" Catalina shrieked.

Jacob stopped just as he was about to step on a mouse sunning itself on the sidewalk.

"Honestly, Jake," she said. "You know how much they love mice here. That could have been the end of your campaign right there."

A scientist with tape on his glasses placed a thimble of lemonade next to the lab mouse and bowed. He gave Jacob a dainty shove and said, "Watch your step, dorkus maximus."

Jacob started to retort, but he didn't imagine the scientist would vote for him if he said something insulting. He forced a smile instead, and said, "Thank you for your kind feedback."

They walked into the museum and suddenly heard an earsplitting scream. "Oh my stars, it's Princess Catalina and Jacob Wonderbar!!" a girl yelled.

A class waiting behind a velvet rope screamed and jumped up and down en masse, pointing and waving. Catalina flashed Jacob a smile and walked over to work the line, laughing, shaking hands, and signing autographs.

Jacob was too surprised to move at first, but he realized that he needed votes and should say hello. He began shaking hands and high-fiving down the line. He was so stunned that the Astral kids knew who he was and were excited to see him that he could barely talk.

"I'm voting for you!" a young boy blurted out when he shook his hand.

"Thanks," Jacob said.

"Ugh," a pigtailed girl grunted. Jacob noticed that

she had hung back and crossed her arms while her classmates were screaming. "I'm not voting for a dirty Earther."

Jacob stopped and stared at her, and she avoided his gaze. He was taken aback by the disgust in her voice and was about to say something when Catalina grabbed him and pulled him away from the line.

"Remember, kids," Catalina announced. "Fashion first! We don't just want your vote, we want you to *look good* while you're voting. Ta-ta for now!"

She pulled Jacob into the next room, which was completely empty. There were some interactive exhibits on the wall and a large, detailed mosaic of Earth on the floor. "I arranged for a private viewing of the museum. You're just lucky I'm leading this tour. Michaelus flunked Astral history three times in a row."

"Shocker," Jacob said.

He wanted to ask her about why the girl in line was so hostile, but an old man with white hair was waving at them. Catalina walked up to him and stuck her hand straight into his chest and then smirked at Jacob's horrified reaction. "Hologram," she said.

Jacob realized that the old man with the crazy white hair looked familiar.

"Albert Einstein," she said. "Have you heard of

him, or did they wipe him from Earther textbooks?"

Jacob sighed. "I've heard of him, yes."

"What they probably didn't teach you in Earther school is that Father Albert built a spaceship and used it to leave Earth behind. He was tired of the Great Earther War and how even though he was the most brilliant Earther in history, all anyone ever wanted him to do was help them build scary horrible weapons. So he grabbed some buddies and left behind a hologram of himself to teach college and keep everyone off his trail. Pretty smart move if you ask me, even if his holo had to avoid shaking people's hands. They just thought he was scared of germs. Meanwhile, the real Albert was off flying around space, exploring planets. He was the first king."

"Wow," Jacob said.

"And guess what?" Catalina spread her arms wide. "I'm a direct descendent! He's my great-great-great-great-great times a million greats grandfather!"

Jacob's eyes went wide at this revelation, but then he chuckled. "Ah. I get it, you're kidding. I'm not that dumb. Albert Einstein wasn't born long enough ago to be your million-times-great-grandfather."

Catalina winked and beckoned Jacob into the next room. "Lesson two. Time travel."

"Time travel?!"

"Oh, Jakey," she said, patting him on the head. "You still haven't figured out what happened when we sent you back to Earth last time? Good thing I'm the brains behind this operation."

Jacob thought back to when the king's scientists put them in the box that sent them back to Earth. They had all thought they would be in a huge amount of trouble after being gone for days, but when they arrived back on Earth no time had elapsed at all and their parents weren't surprised in the slightest to see them. They had wondered what happened but had assumed it was just a consequence of traveling such a great distance, but what actually had happened was . . .

"You didn't just send us back to Earth," he said. "You sent us back in time."

"Such a smart boy," she said. "We know how terribly Earther parents punish their children when they've gone missing. I wouldn't have wanted you to be locked in a box and buried underground for days."

"That's not . . ."

"This way, please."

They stepped into a dark room with a low ceiling that gave Jacob a particularly uneasy feeling.

"Father Albert predicted that Earth would be dangerous to us Astrals someday. Earthers had already spent their first hundred thousand years on the planet

trying to blow each other to bits, and Father Albert said that they would eventually build horrible missiles and try to bring war to space. He knew that he and his friends wouldn't stand a chance in a war since there were just a few Astrals at that time. How could a couple dozen scientists stand up to Earther war machines? So he built a time machine. He wanted Astrals to be ready."

Jacob stared at a device that looked like a coffin with hundreds of cables emitting from it, which was labeled as an early time machine.

"They went back ten thousand years. They multiplied and multiplied and started other space colonies, let some Earthers they trusted join them, and developed new technologies. That's why there are so many of us, scattered on thousands of planets all around the Milky Way galaxy. Now that we're so developed, we're ready for anything Earthers can bring."

Jacob stopped by a monitor showing a black-and-white video of a group of scientists tipping over a sleeping woolly mammoth. They high-fived and danced away, terrifying a nearby caveman, who ran away in fear.

Catalina nodded at the screen. "Sometimes they went back to Earth to visit."

They walked into another room, which had old

faded posters of Earth with X's through it and pictures of planets exploding. Jacob's heart raced. What had poor Earth done to deserve posters showing it blown up or with a thousand missiles pointed at it?

"And that brings us to the Society for Expediting Earther Rapture. It's a movement that thinks we should just blow the whole thing up. Get rid of the Earther threat once and for all. The SEERs have a lot of members and they are a very powerful voting bloc, so we should . . ."

Jacob felt his face go numb. "They want to destroy Earth?! That's why that girl called me a 'dirty Earther'?"

Catalina waved her hand at him. "It's not that nice of a planet."

"You've never even been there!"

The strange things that Jacob had heard Astrals say about Earth were suddenly clicking into place. Officers Bosendorfer and Erard had thought Jacob was the head of an Earther army. The scientists had thought Jacob was stealing the Dragon's Eye to build a weapon. The king had said Astrals were scared of Earth and he had wanted to talk to Jacob to see if he was right that Earth children weren't all bad. And if the king wasn't in power anymore and all of the crazy Astrals could vote on whether to blow up Earth, Jacob was pretty sure he knew which way the vote would go. They didn't take anything seriously, and Jacob suspected they might just blow up Earth on a whim if it struck them as a fun thing to do. All because they had been scared of Earth from the beginning of their history.

Catalina took Jacob's hand and looked him in the eye. He had the sudden sense that he was reacting exactly like she wanted him to, as if she had planned this moment all along. "Listen, Jakey," she said sweetly. "I know you're sentimental about that polluted dustball. And that's why I will make you a deal. When you're elected president, you're going to have a lot of power, including the power to say that there should still be a royal family living on Planet Royale."

Jacob stared into her blue eyes and braced himself for her proposal. She wrung her hands in an unsuccessful attempt to look innocent.

"I'll help you save Earth if you help me stay a princess."

chapter 14

When are we going to find Dexter?" Sarah whispered to Mick. "How much longer do I have to sit through this?"

Mick shushed her, and Sarah turned her attention back to the Planet Valkyrie military demonstration. She had seen enough marching and warship flying and men jumping over walls and climbing ropes to last her several lifetimes. She tapped her foot impatiently as a group of a hundred men marched in order, their arms and legs moving together like identical synchronized robots. Their leader barked a command, and they immediately broke ranks and tumbled into somersaults and cartwheels before they began shooting indiscriminately into the grandstands where Sarah and Mick were sitting. Sarah dove for the floor as blaster shots pinged all around her.

She covered her head and screamed and looked up at Patrick Gravy, who was smiling down at her from his seat. "Isn't it incredible how close they can come to shooting us and still miss?" He shouted, "Deadly marksmanship!"

She looked at Mick, who was smiling along with Patrick, but Sarah could tell he was a bit unsettled. "Good show, Gravy. Now listen, about that—"

"Oh, sir," Patrick interrupted. "You haven't seen the finale. You're going to love this."

Sarah gave Mick a worried look. He flared his eyes a little in understanding, but kept his fake smile plastered on his face.

Patrick pointed in the distance, and though it was daytime, a large moon shone in the Planet Valkyrie sky. There was a rumble nearby, and a giant missile launcher rolled into place on the platform where the Valkyrians had been performing their military exercises.

The missile slowly raised and pivoted until it was pointing directly at the moon.

Patrick offered his Telly to Mick. "Sir, would you like to do the honors?"

90

Mick cleared his throat and said, "There is nothing in the universe that would please me more than destroying a harmless space object that isn't bothering anyone, but I should really decline, since—"

"Great, I'll do it!" Patrick shouted. He quickly punched his Telly with a fat finger and the missile sailed into the sky with a flash of heat and a deafening hiss.

"Mick . . ." Sarah whispered, but he waved her off.

There was a blinding flash of light and Sarah shielded her eyes. When she looked back at the moon it had been replaced by a bright cloud of smoke. Just as the cloud started fading, a thousand shooting stars lit up the Valkyrian atmosphere and pieces of the moon rained down. There was a streak of light nearby and a meteor struck the ground with thundering force, throwing a shower of dust into the air. Sarah dove back down onto the floor and covered her head, praying that a meteor wouldn't hit them.

"Ha-ha!!" Patrick shouted. "I always hated that moon!"

Sarah snuck a glance back up at the sky as the meteors began decreasing in frequency until she finally felt safe to stand up on shaky legs.

As they walked toward the Valkyrie bunker after

the demonstration, Sarah grabbed Mick by the arm and whispered urgently, "These people are terrifying. What are we doing here?"

"We need their endorsement," Mick whispered. "The Valkyrians are very popular. Astrals love explosions, and they're terrified that . . . General Gravy!" he said in greeting as a taller version of Patrick appeared outside of the bunker.

"Candidate Cracken," the man said with a gravelly voice. "I hope you enjoyed the demonstration." He bowed slightly and gestured to the doorway. "Shall we?"

He led them into a dark room with an industrial metal table lit by a single lamp. There were space maps on the walls with military formations drawn in. They sat down around the table and Sarah was reminded of hostage negotiations she had seen in action movies.

"First things first," Mick said. "Where is Dexter Goldstein?"

General Gravy sneered at Patrick, who looked away in embarrassment. "Goldstein has escaped with the space monkeys. They were too clever for my son. He can't help it, he's a very stupid boy."

Patrick's face brightened and he said, "Thanks, Dad!"

General Gravy smiled and patted him on the back proudly. "Takes after his old man."

Mick spread his hands. "Let's get down to business. As you know, I'm—"

"Wait," Sarah interrupted. "What about Dexter? Where did the space monkeys take him?"

Mick pursed his lips and asked grudgingly, "What are we doing about Goldstein?"

"I have it on good authority that Mr. Goldstein is in police custody with Space Officers Bosendorfer and Erard," General Gravy said.

"Thank goodness!" Sarah said. "How do we find him now?"

"Later," Mick said.

"But . . ."

"First we talk business," Mick said. Sarah thought about protesting, but she let it drop. The sooner Mick finished talking to the general, the sooner they'd get off this crazy planet.

"General Gravy," Mick said, "do I have your endorsement?"

The general stood up and began pacing the room. He walked over to one of the space maps and peered at it for a moment, scratching his chin. He carefully moved a blue marker a few inches to the right. He nodded to himself and then turned back to face Sarah and Mick.

"I'll need more weapons systems," General Gravy said, tapping his fingers together in thought. "We've been operating on SEER donations up until this point, but I'll need at least ten percent of the government's budget and official Astral Military status."

"What's 'seer'?" Sarah asked.

Patrick laughed. "The Earther doesn't know what—" But a look from Mick cut him off.

"Ten percent is too much," Mick said. "I need all the money I can spare for bribes. I'll give you five percent and you can be an authorized militia. And I want your word that you will complete Operation Mousetrap. *Successfully* this time."

General Gravy stared at Mick with his best intimidating glare, and Mick just smiled back.

"Fine," General Gravy spat.

Mick stuck out his hand. "So we have a deal?"

General Gravy let Mick stand there with his hand outstretched for a few moments. He scratched his nose and stared at one of his fingernails. "Oh, there's one last thing. I'm sure, given the *value* of the Valkyrian endorsement, you wouldn't hesitate to accept this small request. I would hate for the Astral people to think you don't have their safety in mind."

"What do you want?" Mick said through his teeth.

"If you win, I want authorization to destroy the target of my choosing."

Patrick pounded the table and gave his dad a gleeful fist pump. Mick glanced quickly at Sarah. She was baffled. What target were they talking about?

Mick swallowed and kept his hand outstretched. He gave a faint nod.

"Deal."

Sven, the Planet Royale butler, backed away
from Rufus, who was prancing and baring
his teeth in a threatening fashion. Dexter tried to
get Rufus to calm down, but the chimp didn't like it
when servants entered the room, and he was ready to
defend Dexter with his life.

"Oh my," Sven said. "Nice monkey . . . nice monkey . . . Mr. Goldstein, there's been an incident in the
kitchen. We were hoping you could—"

"An incident?" Dexter jumped up. "I'm coming."

Dexter told Rufus to stay put, but Rufus immediately grabbed him by the leg and made it clear that
Dexter wasn't going anywhere without him. Dexter
finally extricated himself from Rufus and managed
to convince him to stay. He ran with Sven down the

hall and across a courtyard, into a giant kitchen. The monkeys were nowhere to be found, but the entire kitchen was in shambles. There were eggs smashed on the walls, canisters of flour and sugar broken on the floor, dented pots, and banana peels everywhere. The monkeys had destroyed nearly everything.

Dexter found the chef slumped on the floor, his face in his hands. He looked up at Dexter and tears were streaming down his face.

"Chef!" Dexter said, "I'm *so* sorry, I . . ."

"This is the greatest day of my life! The greatest!" the chef cried. He let out a great sniffle and looked at Dexter through gushing tears. He grabbed Dexter's shirt, leaned in, and whispered, "I've never had such an enthusiastic response to my bananas Foster recipe. Never."

"Oh," Dexter said, "so . . . you're not mad?"

The chef looked around at the kitchen and smiled weakly. "I don't know if I shall be this happy ever again."

"Dexter?"

Dexter turned and saw the king of the universe standing in the doorway, his white beard standing out against his gold robes. He was holding Boris's hand, and the grizzled old chimp looked very pleased with himself.

"Can I have a word?"

Dexter's heart thumped in his chest as he followed Boris and the king into the gardens outside of the palace. He saw Mortimer the pink dolphin fly into the air and say, "Hello!"

Dexter hastily shouted, "Hi!" back, knowing Mortimer would continue shouting greetings for hours until he received a response. Mortimer soared into the air and did a belly flop.

"Hey, you!" someone shouted from behind him. Dexter looked up and saw a construction crew sitting on the edge of the roof of the palace, dangling their feet over the side as they ate lunch. The man who shouted held up a large metal lunchbox. "I'm a manly man. That's why I'm yelling at you. I just thought you should know. Are you a manly man?"

Dexter covered his eyes from the sun's glare and said, "No. Not really."

He turned back to follow the king, and the construction worker shouted, "That's right! Keep walking! I knew you were scared!" Dexter shook his head as the construction workers started chanting, "Man-ly men!! Man-ly men!!"

Dexter caught up with the king, who was showing Boris a tree with very smooth bark. Boris slapped the tree and leaned up to see if anything would happen, then quickly scrambled up into the branches. He plucked an acorn from a branch and threw it at Dexter, chirping happily.

"What are the construction workers doing?"

The king turned back to look at the palace as if he was curious to see it still standing there. "It will not be a palace much longer. It will be the seat of the government, and we have to be ready for the new president and representatives to move in."

"But . . ." Dexter started, but the king had turned his back. He walked along the path through the gardens and stopped at a fountain in the shape of an old spaceship. Dexter followed behind him. He wondered why the king was stepping down. He summoned his courage and asked, "What's going to happen to you?"

The king stared down at Dexter for a moment. Dexter made eye contact with him for a brief, terrifying second before he found a pebble on the ground to look at instead.

"What is the one thing you wish you could change about yourself?" the king asked.

"Me?"

"Yes, you."

Dexter thought about the time when Jacob and Sarah had called Maria Garcia and handed him the phone. They had already checked ahead of time to

make sure she would say yes if Dexter asked her to go to the movies, and even though he knew that she would agree, he still couldn't bring himself to say a single word. He hung up in a panic. Sarah screamed bloody murder, Jacob shook his head with a sad grin, and Dexter had made up an excuse about his mom wanting him to sort the recycling and ran home. Dexter wondered if there was a girl somewhere out in the world who would be willing to communicate solely through letters, because he was pretty sure she would be his soul mate.

"I wish I were brave," Dexter said.

The king continued to stare at Dexter and did not betray a hint of feeling. "If I were to give you a potion that would make you the bravest person in the universe, would you take it?"

Dexter recoiled. "You have that?!"

"No." The king smiled. "I don't."

"Oh. Because that would . . ." Dexter trailed off. He thought about suddenly being filled with Jacob Wonderbar–level bravery and finally being able to talk to Maria and getting through the day without being terrified that his mom would make him move his aquarium out of his room in punishment for getting detention. Courage would certainly solve a great number of his problems. But then he also imagined himself getting into trouble all the time and possibly jumping into a fire or performing stunts that would result in disfiguring injuries because he would be too brave to be a highly sensible individual who knew better than to throw himself into certain danger. "I guess I probably wouldn't take it."

The king responded by pressing a piece of green plastic into Dexter's hands.

"What's this?" Dexter asked.

"It's an Astral Telly. You can use it to call anyone in the universe. I think it's time you rejoined your friends."

"Wow." Dexter turned the Telly around in his hands. He had so much to tell Jacob and Sarah about Patrick and the crazy Valkyrians blowing everything up and about how they thought they were kidnapping Jacob Wonderbar and how he called Dexter a dirty Earther and said the king was the only person protecting Earth.

The king turned and started walking away, and Dexter steeled his nerves for one last question. He shouted, "Why did you nominate Jacob for president?"

The king said over his shoulder, "No Astral was brave enough to run against Mick because of his tricks." He paused and turned back to gaze at Dexter directly. "But mainly because the survival of Planet Earth depends on it."

Dexter felt a shiver down his spine to hear his worst fears about Patrick and the Valkyrians confirmed. He had to warn Jacob to make sure he knew how important it was to win the election. It was a matter of planetary life and death.

Dexter heard a screech. He turned back to the palace and saw Rufus scramble over a balcony and bound toward him. He turned away and braced himself as Rufus launched himself into the air and plowed Dexter into the ground.

"I wasn't going to leave without you!" he said as the chimp buried his face in Dexter's back.

chapter 16

Jacob stared at his Telly for a long time in the darkness aboard Praiseworthy. He was resting in bed on his way to a campaign event in a distant region of the galaxy. He had watched enough ANN that he was growing used to being whisked in and out of news stories, but after listening to two commentators yell at each other for fifteen minutes about whether Mick Cracken was going to receive 90 percent of the vote or 95 percent, he'd had enough and shouted, "Off!"

He knew his campaign was foundering and that he should probably call it off and admit defeat. The Astrals were hostile to Earthers, and as much as he tried to assure them they were wrong about Earth, he couldn't convince them to vote for him.

But there was some part of him deep down that refused to give up, not when it meant losing to Mick Cracken and not before he had given it everything he had. He still had Catalina, and even if she had her own agenda, at least she knew the Astrals and what they wanted.

Sometimes Jacob even pictured his dad watching him be named president of the universe, and he wondered what his dad would feel in that moment. He wasn't sure whether he wanted his dad to be proud of him or whether he wanted him to be sad, to be forced to admit that he had been wrong about Jacob and was wrong to have left him behind. He wasn't sure what being elected president would prove to himself or his dad, but he knew it would mean something. He knew he had to run even if it meant certain defeat.

He stared at the phone. There was still something that wasn't right.

"Call Sarah Daisy," he said to the Telly.

The phone rang for a long time. He waited, hoping she would pick up, and then suddenly he was inside another spaceship. He looked around. He was in a bedroom. The walls were all painted black, and there were graffiti paintings on the wall in gold frames. Sarah was sitting on a bed in the middle of the room, holding a lavender Telly and looking over at Jacob wistfully. The bed was also covered in a lavender comforter.

"Mick's idea of a joke, I think," she said quietly. "He knows I hate lavender."

Jacob stared at her. He couldn't believe that she had actually joined Mick's campaign and was working against him.

"Who are you talking to?" he heard Mick's voice say.

Sarah scowled and shouted, "I'm on the Telly, and if you tell Mick about this, I swear I'll stick a fork straight in your hard drive. Don't think I won't do it!"

"Who was that?" Jacob asked. "That was Mick?"

"Mick Jr.," she said. "Mick programmed his nav system with his own personality."

Jacob couldn't help but grin. "You have to deal with two of them?"

Sarah smiled faintly. "You should hear it when they argue with each other."

Jacob laughed and then stopped and stared at his feet for a moment. They caught each other's eye and then both looked away.

Sarah stared at the wall. "Why didn't you go back for Dexter? If you had just gone back for him none of this would have happened."

"Oh I see," Jacob said. "Kind of like how you

stranded Dexter and me on Numonia last time? You're one to talk. Every time something happens, you go running off with Mick Cracken."

Sarah shook her head. "It's not about Mick," she said.

"Sure it isn't."

Sarah threw aside the covers and stood up. "What about you and Princess Pointyhead?! Every time that alien shows up you go all weak in the knees. You should have seen the look on your face when she walked into the room on Planet Headline."

"That's not true."

"'Can I call you Cat?'" she said in an exaggerated Jacob Wonderbar impression. "'No? *Princess* Cat? Whatever you want, darling! I'll follow your stupid personality anywhere because you're so beautiful.'"

Jacob felt the blood rushing between his ears and he thought about saying, "End call" and leaving Mick's ship, but he stood rooted to his spot. "I have to do this," he said quietly. "It was hard, but I had to leave Dexter behind and I had to make Catalina my running mate. It was my only shot at winning."

"Winning," Sarah said with a sour expression. "I'm going to make sure you lose. So things will go back to how they were."

And with that, Jacob knew why she'd run off with Mick. He remembered their conversation on the curb before they blasted off to space, how worried she was about him winning and everything changing and never being able to see each other. Sarah just wanted to go back to Earth so everything would go back to normal. A part of him even understood where she was coming from.

He stepped closer and reached for her, but his hand passed straight through hers. They weren't there in the same room, it was all an illusion created by the Tellys. They were billions of miles apart, on different

ships, sailing through different parts of the galaxy on separate campaigns.

"Come back," Jacob said.

"I'm sorry, Jake," she said quietly. "I can't."

Jacob glared at her for a moment and said, "End call."

chapter 17

Jacob was in a bad mood even before Catalina told him about his first campaign assignment. He awoke from a fitful sleep when they arrived on Planet Hermit, which was named in honor of the planet's only resident: Roy Blankwell, one of the most popular talk show hosts in outer space. Jacob put on the suit that Catalina picked out for him, a black suit lined with small sparkling electronic lights that made him feel like a human disco ball.

"Blankwell is very influential," Catalina said. "If you impress him we can make serious headway."

"So what do I have to do?"

Catalina rolled her eyes. "Oh Jakey, don't go worrying yourself. I know you'll nail it."

"He's really the only person on this planet? Why is his show so popular?"

Catalina found something interesting to stare at on her Telly. "I'm sorry, what did you say? Would you hurry? It's almost time."

Praiseworthy had parked on a ledge near the top of a massive mountain. Jacob stepped out of the ship and stared down into the deepest canyon he had ever seen. Jagged brown peaks jutted up in the distance and colorful giant birds soared in between them. Jacob walked with Catalina toward Blankwell's house, which was perched at the very top of a high mountain, its walls stark white and formidable.

After Blankwell buzzed them in, Catalina pushed Jacob through a giant marble entryway and into a studio that was set up as a living room, with a purple couch and a painting of a spaceship on the wall. An older man with a pleasant face was sitting behind a gleaming white desk, and he beamed when Jacob came into the room. He was wearing an impeccable purple suit that matched the couch, and it shimmered under the lights in the studio. Jacob was suddenly aware that he was being recorded and there were likely millions of Astrals tuned in at that very moment.

"Mr. Wonderbar!" Blankwell said. "Please, have a seat. I should have known you'd be late."

"I'm late?"

"Slow brains, I see," Blankwell chuckled. Jacob tried not to frown at the insult and wondered if Blankwell had just misfired on a joke. Blankwell looked at some note cards and gestured around to an invisible audience. "Mr. Wonderbar, why don't you start off telling my viewing friends whether your worst quality is your horrible temper or the unfortunate sound of your voice?"

"What?!"

"Horrible temper it is. I had a feeling."

"I don't have a horrible—"

"Oh, so you aren't *aware* you have a horrible temper?"

Jacob stared at the smiling talk show host and realized what was going on. Blankwell wanted to get a rise out of Jacob so that he would say something stupid. Jacob cleared his throat, gave a faint grin, and said, "We all have our weaknesses."

"You just happen to have more weaknesses than most, wouldn't you agree?"

"Oh, I wouldn't say—"

"Your campaign started off with what is widely agreed to be the worst speech in the history of the universe. Really dreadful stuff. How do you plan to rescue your campaign so you receive more than one

111

vote? Sources tell me your running mate herself is on the fence about whether to vote for you."

Jacob wondered for a fleeting moment if that was true about Catalina, but just when he realized Blankwell was lying it was too late and the host pounced. "Hesitating because it's true? So your campaign manager really isn't going to vote for you?"

"It's not true, I—"

"I thought so," Blankwell purred. "Confirmed by Candidate Wonderbar himself."

Jacob grabbed the armrest of his chair hard enough that his knuckles were white. He told himself to calm down and look for an opening.

Blankwell looked at his cards and adopted a pained expression. "Your own best friend deserted your campaign. Had to have been a shock. Would you care to comment on reports that Sarah Daisy and Mick Cracken are in love?"

Jacob swallowed against his knotted throat, and said confidently, "What I think the voters want to hear about are the issues in this campaign. For instance, Astral time makes no sense at all. What I want to talk about is—"

"I think they are definitely in love," Blankwell interrupted.

"—is what I can do to help out the Astral people. I think they might be surprised—"

"Completely in love."

"—at what I can bring, because I am someone who is honest and well-intentioned—"

"Probably kissing right now."

"—which is more than I can say about my opponent, whose only qualification is that he's a pretend pirate who does nothing but lie, wouldn't you agree with me, Mr. Blankwell?"

Blankwell stared at Jacob in surprise for a moment and Jacob seized on his hesitation. "How long have Astrals had democracy?" Jacob asked.

Blankwell frowned. "I ask the questions on this show, and—"

"The answer is you still don't have it because you haven't even voted. We've had it on Earth for, um . . ." Jacob tried to remember what Ms. Rao had said about democracy in World History. "Well, we've had it for a long time, and I know how it works. Astrals don't know everything, believe it or not."

"Let's get back to the real issue of this campaign," Blankwell said, regaining his footing. "You have already admitted that you are an Earther secret agent sent here to undermine—"

"That is so wrong," Jacob said, but before he could say anything further, Catalina rushed into the studio.

"You're in danger!" she shouted. "Valkyrians have landed outside."

Jacob briefly wondered whether this was one of Catalina's campaign stunts, but Blankwell jumped up in a panic before he seemed to remember he was on camera and made a show of adjusting his tie. "Ha. Guess I shouldn't have told that joke about how many Valkyrians it takes to turn on a spaceship." He paused as if waiting for a laugh.

Jacob stared at Blankwell in confusion. "Huh?"

"The answer is minus two, because at least two of them would blow themselves up in the process."

"No, what's that word? What are Valkyrians?"

Catalina said, "SEERs, Jake. SEERs with blasters."

"They want to destroy Earth? What are they doing here?"

Catalina grabbed his hand. "We have to run."

chapter 18

Jacob started running toward the door they'd come in, but Catalina grabbed him and whispered, "No. There has to be another way out."

They heard a crash and the sound of boots echoing from the entryway. Jacob felt a shove from behind, and Blankwell went running past them, up a nearby stairwell, and down a hallway.

Jacob and Catalina looked at each other and then went running after him.

"Target spotted!" someone shouted from behind them.

Jacob glanced over his shoulder and saw a blond-haired kid in a uniform aiming a blaster at him. Jacob dove to the ground as the wall cracked behind him, leaving a smoking spot where it hit.

"I said no lethal force!" a deeper voice said.

"Oh. Sorry, Dad."

"That's all right, son. It's not your fault the Earther deserves it."

Catalina grabbed a gold vase from the wall and threw it in the direction of the soldiers, and then helped Jacob up, pulling him down a white marble hallway. "The Gravys," she whispered. "General Gravy is the leader of the Valkyrians, and Patrick is his son. This is very bad."

"Why are they chasing us?"

"I don't know, but we need to hurry."

They rounded a corner and found yet another white marble hallway, but this time Blankwell was waiting for them. He stood with his arms crossed and a mischievous look on his face.

"Blankwell, you have to help us," Catalina said.

He smiled cryptically. "Any last words for the viewers, *Princess*?"

Jacob glanced quickly at Catalina and knew that Blankwell had infuriated her with the mere inflection of his voice. At any other time Blankwell would have had to follow her orders and bow to her every whim, knowing she might be the future queen. He wouldn't have dared make fun of her directly. But now she was just the running mate on a losing presidential cam-

paign, and he could sneer at her and get away with it. Jacob had a feeling she'd never been treated that way in her entire life.

"I'll remember this," she said quietly.

Blankwell punched a button on the wall and Jacob felt the ground give way. He and Catalina were sliding through a dark tunnel, twisting and turning as they gained speed. Jacob saw light ahead, and before he could brace himself he was thrown onto the ground. Catalina fell on top of him. He strained to breathe and did a mental inventory of his limbs, and though he was definitely bruised, he was pretty sure he hadn't broken anything.

Catalina hopped to her feet, and Jacob stood up gingerly. They were on a small ledge atop a sheer cliff, and Jacob turned to look around just as the door to the slide slammed shut. Catalina stared at her Telly, but shook her head. "Praiseworthy isn't answering."

"What do we do now?" he asked.

Jacob was suddenly thrown back to the ground and he felt the heat of an explosion. As the ringing of his ears died down he heard loud cheers, and he saw a group of Valkyrian soldiers readying another grenade launch on a distant cliff.

"We have to get out of here!" Jacob shouted.

He stared down into the chasm at the edge of the

cliff, where some of the massive birds that he'd seen earlier were flying. They looked like falcons the size of whales and each one was a different color, bright green and red and yellow. One of the birds swooped high near him, and he stood back from the cliff as it passed them, so close he could feel the air stir around him.

Jacob had an idea. If he could just time it right, he could leap off the cliff onto one of their backs and fly to safety.

"We can do this. We can jump onto the birds," Jacob said. "I'll go first."

He took a few steps back, just far enough so he could see the birds swirling around, and prepared to launch himself off the cliff.

"Jake . . ." Catalina sighed. "Don't jump!" She pointed at the corner of the ledge, where he saw the top of a ladder.

"Oh."

They scrambled over to the ladder and began climbing down, holding on as best they could. He clung tightly to the ladder whenever the Valkyrians launched grenades into the ravine. The birds squawked angrily, but they managed to dodge the blasts.

After it seemed as if they had climbed for an eternity, Catalina suddenly stopped.

"Um. Jake?"

Jacob moved his left leg so he could look down at her, and then felt a stab of panic. They had reached the end of the ladder, but they were still hundreds of feet in the air. There was nothing but clouds beneath them, and there was surely no way they could climb back up without being killed or captured by the Valkyrians.

Jacob wondered if his leaping-onto-birds idea was now a bit more viable.

He heard a buzzing sound growing closer, and a small vehicle rose up through the clouds. The smaller Gravy was riding a flying motorcycle, and he swung up alongside Jacob and Catalina. He hovered there for a moment with a dumb grin.

"Hi," Gravy said. "Just hanging out? Ha-ha! Get it? Hanging out? Because you're hanging on to that ladder there? Holy stars I'm funny sometimes."

Jacob's fingers were beginning to ache from holding on to the ladder, and he hadn't noticed the strength of the wind, which was tugging at his suit and sending a shiver down his spine.

"Gravy, darling, cutie-pie," Catalina said sweetly, in a voice Jacob realized had been directed at him many times. "What might I be able to offer your hilarious bad self to rescue us and let us get back to our campaign? Hmm?"

Gravy laughed, which Jacob thought sounded a bit like an old car honking. "Oh, it's too late for that, Princess Catalina. Your brother has already given us exactly what we want."

Catalina gasped. "He did what?!"

"This election is over. All I have to do is kidnap you and—"

Jacob clenched his jaw. "Mick Cracken sent you to kidnap us?" he said angrily.

The grin on Patrick's face evaporated,

and he pointed his blaster at Jacob. "I didn't say that."

"Yes, you did."

Patrick clenched his jaw, and Jacob noted that his hand was shaking.

Jacob heard a strange noise that he thought sounded like a proper "Yee-haw" echoing around the ravine, and he saw a flash of orange out of the corner of his eye. Jacob turned and saw Praiseworthy speeding toward them. Patrick's eyes went wide in fear and he fired some shots at Praiseworthy, but when the ship didn't alter course Patrick tipped up his motorcycle and fled. Praiseworthy was going so fast Jacob thought he was going to crash into the mountain, but just before he reached the cliff face he came to a sudden, perfect stop.

They were saved.

chapter 19

Catalina danced around her ship as Praiseworthy left the Valkyrians far behind. "Thank you, Praiseworthy! Thank you, thank you! You're the best! I knew you liked me more than Mick!"

"Oh Princess Catalina, you wouldn't believe the adventure I had. I just knew I had one good rollicking rescue in me!"

Jacob smiled and wished he could give Praiseworthy a high five. "What happened? How did you escape the Valkyrians?"

"Well," Praiseworthy said, quite obviously beside himself that they wanted to hear his story, "when I heard that nasty brute of a Valkyrian spaceship enter the atmosphere I just knew it couldn't be good news. So I left right that moment, flew below the cloud line, hid behind a mountain, and shut off all communications so I couldn't possibly be spotted. I knew you may have been unable to reach me, but I couldn't dare take the risk of having our conversation intercepted. And after I saw that horrible gremlin of a child speed by me on his motorcycle, I just knew he would lead me to you. It *was* a magnificent rescue, wasn't it?"

"It was!" Catalina said. She twirled around one more time and ran over and hugged Jacob. He hugged her back and was proud that they had escaped. Catalina was smarter and braver than he had given her credit for, and he was glad they were campaigning together.

But then he had a flash of what Sarah Daisy would have done if she had seen him hug Catalina, and a part of him wondered if this was all part of Catalina's plan, whether she just thought he would be easily wrapped around her finger. She was a member of the same family as Mick Cracken after all.

"Your dad said that Astrals are all fun-loving people, that space is perfect and all that. So why were they trying to kill me? They want to destroy Earth! What kind of maniacs are you people?"

Catalina broke the hug and took a few steps back, looking genuinely hurt. Her mouth was a thin line and she nodded. "Jacob," she said quietly, "SEERs

are crazy. They just love blowing things up. Not all Astrals are like that."

"Didn't you say they're popular?"

"Well, yes, kind of, but you know . . . Astrals just don't take things so . . . *seriously*."

She gave him a look that made him think she was talking about more than just Astrals.

"Dexter Goldstein calling!" Jacob's Astral Telly shouted.

Jacob reached into his pocket and saw Dexter's face. He was safe. Jacob quickly said, "Pick up," and Dexter materialized right in front of him. He had a vague sense that Catalina let out a sniffle and brushed past him toward her stateroom, but he was too excited about seeing Dexter to worry about it.

"Dexter!" Jacob shouted. "What happened to you?"

Dexter looked around and said, "Whoa! You're aboard Praiseworthy? Hi, Praiseworthy! Hi!!"

Jacob shook his head. "That's not how the Tellys work. Only I can hear you."

"Oh. Weird."

"Hey Praiseworthy," Jacob said. "Dexter says hi."

"Master Goldstein!" Praiseworthy shouted. "My warmest regards! I daresay you would have been quite impressed by my recent dashing rescue!"

Jacob thought back to the last time he had seen

Dexter, being carried away by space monkeys, and he felt a wave of guilt that he had left his friend behind. Jacob had only sent crazy space officers to save him and had taken his election more seriously than his friend's rescue. He looked at the ground and said, "Look. Dexter. I really, really wish I could have come back for you. I just had that deadline to declare my candidacy, and . . ."

Dexter stood a little straighter. "I can take care of myself," he said, as if he were testing the words out to see how they sounded. He cocked his head a little and then nodded as if they sounded just fine.

"Well, still, I'm sorry, Dexter," Jacob said

Dexter nodded. "I am a brave individual."

Jacob laughed. "I can tell. How did you escape the space monkeys?"

"Escape?" Dexter looked around the room. "You can't see them?"

Jacob shook his head. "Dexter, that's not how these phones work. The caller goes to where the recipient of the call is, and their image—"

"Yeah, yeah. Well, they're right here beside me and they're my friends!"

Jacob wondered if Dexter had possibly suffered a catastrophic head injury during his ordeal. He certainly did not sound like the Dexter he knew. It

occurred to him that the space monkeys could have been holding Dexter hostage and were forcing him to say he was fine and pretend he was self-sufficient under threat of further space monkey rampage.

"Wow, Dex," he said. "That's, um, great. But really, are you okay?"

Dexter's eyes widened as if he were just realizing something. "Earth is in danger! There are these lunatics called Valkyrians . . ."

"Yeah, I met some of them."

"Oh. Well, that's who I rescued the space monkeys from. I think they meant to kidnap *you*."

"Wait," Jacob said. Pieces were beginning to fit together. "So the Valkyrians sent the space monkeys to kidnap me, only they grabbed you instead. Then they tried to get me again just now. And Patrick Gravy—"

"I hate that guy!" Dexter shouted.

"Me too!" Jacob said. "He said something about Mick giving the Valkyrians what they wanted."

"They want to destroy Earth! The king said he nominated you because you were the only one who could save Earth!"

Jacob couldn't believe Mick had sent a bunch of Earth-hating goons to kidnap him, but he was still a bit proud to hear that the king wanted him to save Earth. "I knew Mick was the one who sent the Valky-

rians to kidnap me! So he would win without a contest."

Dexter nodded. "That makes sense! Stupid Mick!"

Jacob was incredibly relieved that Dexter was safe and wasn't mad, and he was so glad he would have him along for the rest of the election. Together they had defeated every obstacle substitute teachers had thrown at them, and he knew they could conquer the universe when they rejoined forces.

"So you're really friends with the space monkeys?" Jacob asked.

"Yes." Dexter nodded. "I really am. I'm like their king."

Jacob started to laugh, thinking Dexter was joking, but when he saw that Dexter was serious he stopped himself.

"Well, bring them along," Jacob said. "I need some security guards."

chapter 20

We need a better slogan," Mick said as he threw a ball against the wall and caught it. He stopped and then held up his hands like a magician. "The Truth Crusader. No, that's not right. Hmm . . . Let's see . . . Truth and Justice. Truth and . . . something. Definitely need to have *truth* in there somewhere."

Sarah wondered for the seven hundredth time what she was doing riding around on a Mick Cracken–designed spaceship campaigning to elect him president of the universe. The food was terrible (Mick considered an Astral version of Sloppy Joes one of the five food groups), the company was insufferable, and she had heard enough lounge music to last her several lifetimes. Given how poorly Jacob had run his campaign so far, she had no doubt she and

Mick would win, but that didn't make his constant antics any easier to deal with.

They were headed for Planet Veritas, the place where Astrals had their court system and where it was strictly forbidden to tell a single lie, no matter how large or small. Sarah couldn't begin to fathom why Mick Cracken of all people had agreed to debate Jacob on a planet where he was legally bound to tell the entire truth, but he'd insisted that it would be good for the campaign.

She stared at Mick and wondered how many brain cells he really had left. "I thought you promised everyone you were going to lie all the time," she said. "Why are we doing this?"

Sarah knew that Mick would bestow on her a smug grin in response, his expression of choice whenever she questioned one of his devious schemes. Sure enough, he smiled exactly like she thought he would. Somehow the fact that she knew in advance that he would smile like that made her even angrier.

"Oh Sarah, so much to learn, so much to learn," Mick said. "Slogans aren't about *lying*. Here's what you do. You take one of your weaknesses and say the exact opposite, but in a way that's not technically lying. Watch. If you were very short, you'd say, 'Standing Tall for Astrals!' You're not saying you *are* tall, just that you're *standing* as tall as you can even though you're tiny. If you were the head of an Earther company that accidentally turned a river purple, you'd say, 'Protecting the Environment One River at a Time!' That line is genius because the one river you were protecting at that time wasn't the one you turned purple."

"And what should my slogan be?"

Mick caught the ball he had been bouncing and thought silently for a second. Sarah hoped his brain didn't blow a fuse. Then he grinned and said, "Sarah Daisy: She'll Grow on You if You Get to Know Her Better."

"What's that supposed to mean?!"

"Genius, sir," Mick Jr. chimed in.

"Oh, well of course you'd agree with him," Sarah spat.

Mick adopted a concerned expression, and Sarah braced herself for some flattery. "You know you're an Earther, right? Astrals are a little suspicious of people from your planet, in case you haven't noticed. But they'll love you once they look past all that."

Sarah tried to decide if he was being sincere or was still making fun of her. "I guess I can see that."

"Trust me, I know what it feels like when people underestimate you." He stared into the distance and

Sarah thought she saw a hint of sadness in Mick's face. "My own dad nominated someone else for president. How do you think that felt?"

It had never even occurred to her that when the king threw his weight behind Jacob's candidacy, he was undermining his own son's dreams. It was Mick's idea to have a president in the first place, and yet his own dad didn't think he was capable of it. She felt a pang of sympathy. Sarah's parents thought she was capable of anything.

"Sir," Mick Jr. said. "We've arrived on Planet Veritas."

"About time too," Mick said, smiling again at Sarah. He gave her a wave as if what they had been talking about was nothing to worry about. "The perfect place for my new campaign slogan. 'Striving for Truth, and a Running Mate Who Is Really Kind of Nice, No Really, You Should Go Bowling with Her Sometime.'"

"You're impossible," Sarah said as she walked with Mick toward the rear of the ship.

They were met by a very stern old man in bright red robes, along with a rotund space officer who fiddled with his handcuffs like he was itching to arrest someone. The man in red robes promptly held up his right hand and said, "Do you swear to tell the whole truth the entire time you are on Planet Veritas and agree that any lie will be met with immediate imprisonment?"

"Yes," Sarah said, glancing in fear at the space officer.

"Absolutely," Mick said.

"In order to enter our planet, your commitment to the sanctity of truth must be tested. What is the ugliest part of my face?" the man asked. He pointed at Sarah. "You first."

Sarah's eyes went wide. Was she really supposed to tell this man a part of his face was ugly? She didn't want to hurt his feelings or make him mad. But she didn't want to go to prison for lying either. Her heart raced and she said very carefully, "Well, I mean, you're a very, um . . ." She was about to say *handsome,* but she realized it wasn't true. "*Distinguished*-looking person, and while I'd hate to say anything bad about your face . . . Which is true! Um, since I have to pick something out . . ." Sarah closed her eyes. "Your hairy mole. I'm so sorry!"

She opened her eyes and the man nodded. He didn't seem to be offended.

He turned to Mick and said, "And what's the most unpleasant part of being around—"

"Bad breath," Mick said immediately. "Like, really, insanely bad. You should get that checked out."

The man nodded again. "Quite right. You may enter our planet." He bowed politely and walked away. Sarah wasn't so sure she wanted to step off the ship.

Mick, on the other hand, jumped in the air and pumped his fist. "I love it here!"

chapter 21

The man in red robes, whose name was Mr. Simon, cleared a piece of phlegm from his throat and then reminded everyone that the candidates were under oath to tell the truth and the whole truth or else they would be locked up in a most unpleasant jail. Jacob stood smugly behind his lectern while Mick checked out his hair in a small mirror. There was no way Mick could beat him at a debate where honesty was a requirement.

Jacob looked out into the crowd and saw Sarah Daisy, and he narrowed his eyes at her. She narrowed her eyes back. He was even more motivated to win the debate.

"Now then," Mr. Simon said. "What do you feel

are the most important issues in the campaign? Let's start with Candidate Wonderbar."

Jacob turned to the audience and cameras and said, "Thank you, Mr. Simon. Let's start with time, which is completely confusing. I don't know how anyone can tell their zoomecs from their parcelticks from their starweeks. Different planets have different time systems, and that doesn't make sense. When I'm president I'll start an initiative to fix that. One Galaxy, One Time. It's time"—Jacob smiled at his pun—"for a change."

The audience clapped politely. Mick yawned.

"Candidate Cracken?" Mr. Simon prompted.

"Wouldn't some say that the biggest issue in the campaign is that my opponent is deranged and possibly a former mental patient?" Mick asked.

Jacob smiled and stuck a finger out at Mick. "That's a lie! Arrest him!"

The audience stirred and chattered, and Mr. Simon called for order.

Mick raised his hands in innocence. "Oh, *I* wouldn't say that my opponent is a deranged psychopath. I believe Candidate Wonderbar is an upstanding citizen who knows how to tie his shoes. I'm just asking a *question*, and a question isn't a lie. Should people be worried that Jacob Wonderbar could be completely crazy and mentally imbalanced? Should they be terrified of his secret agenda? Those are just questions, understand."

Jacob felt his ears burning. Mick had found a loophole.

"Should people be worried that my opponent is a liar who can't tell the truth?" Jacob asked.

"No, they shouldn't," Mick said. "Because we're on a planet where I am legally bound to tell the truth. If I lied, I would be imprisoned."

Jacob fumed. He had thought that Mick would be slowed down on Planet Veritas, but he realized Mick was just using the planet against him. Still, he knew the worst thing he could do would be to fall into Mick's plot. He needed to stick to his game plan.

"Let's get back to the issues," Jacob said. "There is not nearly enough pizza in outer space, and if I were president—"

"Did you see how Candidate Wonderbar just interrupted me?" Mick asked.

"But . . ." Jacob sputtered. "You just interrupted *me*! I was trying to—"

"Sad, isn't it?" Mick asked. "Makes you wonder . . ."

Jacob turned back to Mr. Simon in exasperation and waited for him to ask another question.

"Why do you want to be president?" Mr. Simon asked. "Candidate Cracken, you first."

Mick rested his chin on a fist, appearing deep in thought, and then said, "This election was my idea. I convinced the king, my father, that the people deserved to choose their own leader. That is why you now have the right to vote. I think having a monarchy is lazy"—he looked up as he said this, and Jacob knew he was making a point of looking at Catalina—"and I think this election is the best thing to ever happen to the Astral people. We can decide our future together. I know I'm the right person to lead us into this new era."

As the audience applauded, Jacob waited a moment for police to swoop in to arrest Mick, but he realized he must not have been lying.

"Candidate Wonderbar?" Mr. Simon asked. "Why do you want to be president?"

Jacob wanted to come up with something just as eloquent as Mick's response, to give the people the answer they wanted to hear, something that sounded even more impressive. But he knew he couldn't so much as stretch the truth, or else he'd land in jail. And the truth wasn't impressive at all.

He looked down at the lectern and said, "I think I'd do a good job. And . . . well, the king asked me to."

And with that, Jacob knew that the truth had just cost him the debate.

chapter 22

Jacob tried to get some rest as they blasted off from Planet Veritas, but all he could do was stare at his Telly. He had successfully survived a Valkyrian kidnapping attempt, his debate was a disaster, and he was very, very tired. He thought about ending it all and just heading back to the tunnel through the space kapow and back home to the street where all the houses looked the same. Maybe being king of the seventh grade was really all he was cut out for.

Even still, he couldn't quite give up on his dream. He wasn't sure if his Telly would work back on Earth, and there was someone he needed to summon the courage to call before he decided to go home. He could find out once and for all if his dad really was in outer space and talk to him and—

There was a loud banging on his door. Jacob sat up quickly.

"Who is it?"

"Can I come in?" Catalina shouted from outside.

Jacob slumped back onto his pillow. "Fine."

Catalina skipped into the room and thrust her Telly in his face. "Good news! Your poll numbers have finally moved. We're at twenty percent! The debate didn't hurt us *too* much, and people loved our escape on Planet Hermit."

"Really?"

Catalina smiled with pride. "They thought you conducted yourself like a true Astral."

Jacob wondered how running for your life and being saved by a spaceship constituted acting like an Astral. "I conducted myself like a human being," he mumbled.

"Well, they didn't know you could be so . . . *exciting*. This is exactly where we want to be heading into the Battles Supreme! Everyone loves a comeback, and if we could just get your poll numbers peaking at the right time, we'll—"

"Wait. The Battles what?"

"The Battles Supreme," Catalina said.

"Oh, right. What are those?"

"Oh . . . wow. Darling, do you even *have* news on

Earth? The Battles Supreme. Three tests of intelligence and strength so everyone can make up their minds before voting day. The battles are judged by the Election Council, except for the third one, which is judged by my daddy. The first one involves corndogs."

"Corndogs? Really?" Jacob had imagined himself swinging from ropes and jumping over logs like he had seen in military training scenes. He wasn't sure how leaping across a muddy pond would make him qualified to be president, but he had stopped being surprised about anything Astral-related.

Jacob suddenly remembered that Catalina had been upset with him for being so rude about her hugging him and for lumping her in with the Valkyrians even though she wasn't like them. And yet there she was standing before him looking rested and happy as if she didn't have a care in the world. He admired that she never seemed to let anything get her down for long, and she appeared genuinely excited that they had made some progress on their campaign. But that didn't change the fact that he had been rude.

"Hey," Jacob said. "Catalina. Sorry about calling Astrals maniacs, I—"

"Shush!" Catalina said. She shook her head and beamed. "You don't ever have to apologize to me."

Jacob frowned. Whenever he crossed Sarah Daisy,

things were never better until he had groveled out apologies until he couldn't grovel any more and had thoroughly exhausted every drop of pride and patience he possessed, at which time she maybe, possibly found it in her better self to forgive him. It didn't seem right that Catalina wouldn't let him apologize, let alone *expect* him to try to make amends. "But that's . . . I don't think that's how it's supposed to work."

Catalina waved her finger at him. "Shush, shush, shush. You just worry about winning this election."

"But—"

"Ta, darling!"

Catalina skipped out of his room and closed the door behind her. Jacob wondered if he would someday come to understand the workings of the female mind.

"Oh my!" Praiseworthy shouted. "We have trouble."

Jacob heard a noise at the rear of the ship. He jumped out of bed and ran toward the hold. He heard a galloping sound and suddenly a large gray-haired chimpanzee ran past him, slipped on the smooth floor, and crashed into a wall.

"No! Boris! Inside running, please!" Dexter shouted.

Jacob reached the hold and found Dexter surrounded by monkeys and a small one clinging to his back.

"We made it!" Dexter said.

Jacob walked over and high-fived Dexter. He was so glad they were finally back together.

"What did I miss?" Dexter asked.

Jacob felt many different emotions all at once when he thought back to the last week and all the things Dexter had missed. He tried to figure out what he should tell Dexter first. When he had last seen Dexter, Jacob thought he was a shoo-in and had assumed since the king nominated him that the election would just be a formality. But instead he had given poorly received speeches and had nearly been chased to his death and lost to Mick in a debate. "I don't know, Dexter," he said finally. "This has been hard."

"Harder than surviving Numonia?"

Jacob thought back to eating space dust, and it made him smile a little. "Yeah. Even harder than that."

Dexter peered at Jacob as if he had been replaced by a robot, and Jacob realized that he couldn't remember a time when he was scared and Dexter was the confident one. He felt like the ground was shifting beneath him.

Dexter slapped Jacob on the back. "Cheer up, Wonderbar. If I can escape a bunch of crazy soldiers and rescue a clan of space monkeys, I'm pretty sure it means you can do anything. The king nominated you to save Earth. You have to win."

Jacob felt some blood returning to his face. Dexter was right. Failure wasn't an option.

"But don't do it for me," Dexter said. "Do it for the monkeys."

chapter 23

Sarah watched as Mr. Simon prepared for his post-debate interview with Mick, who looked serene and content and right at home. Sarah just wanted him to get it over with so they could leave. She was quite fed up with the matter-of-fact honesty of the Veritasians. She had already been told that she was overly intense, that her clothes were horribly out of style, and Mr. Simon had proclaimed that he didn't particularly like children. There was a reason normal people don't tell every truth, Sarah reasoned, and it was because having all of your flaws pointed out all the time was not a recipe for healthy self-esteem.

"Well," Mr. Simon said to Mick, "I don't mind telling you I had a rather disgusting visit with the stomach doctor this morning."

"What's the prognosis?" Mick asked, as if it were a perfectly normal line of conversation for a presidential interview.

"Smelly," Mr. Simon said. "Now then. Let's discuss your personality. The people would like to know which is your weakest quality as a potential president."

Mick smiled. "That depends on what you mean by the word 'weakest.'"

Mr. Simon looked a bit confused. "You don't know what the word 'weakest' means?"

Mick adopted a very patient expression. "Of course I know what it means, but how do I know that you know what it means?"

Sarah realized that Mick had found yet another Planet Veritas loophole. He was a master of nonsense, and nonsense was not necessarily a lie.

"Let's just say," Mr. Simon said, "that my definition of 'weakest' is the same as your definition of 'weakest.' And might I remind you, Mr. Cracken, that you are under oath to tell the whole truth."

Mick let a pause stretch on. "Well then, I'd definitely say cornflakes."

Mr. Simon blinked. "Cornflakes are your weakest quality?"

"Yes." Mick nodded.

"Why?"

"Why what?" Mick asked.

Even Sarah was beginning to want to punch Mick, and she could tell that Mr. Simon shared the sentiment.

"Why are cornflakes your weakest quality?" Mr. Simon asked.

"Why do *you* think cornflakes are my weakest quality?" Mick asked.

Mr. Simon stared at Mick, and Sarah sensed that he was reconsidering his line of questioning. Mick looked perfectly thrilled with himself.

Mr. Simon shuffled some papers and scowled at Mick. "I'm going to invoke Article Seven of the Veritas Constitution and insist that you answer a series of yes or no questions completely honestly. Failure to comply or any lying will result in immediate imprisonment. Do you understand?"

Mick nodded and reclined in his chair as if he were on vacation. "Yes."

"Do you think you will be a better president than Candidate Wonderbar?"

"Absolutely," Mick said.

"Are your days as a space pirate behind you and will you pledge to uphold the law of the land?"

"Nope."

"Will you put the greater good ahead of your own personal self-interest?"

Mick's eyes glinted. "Yes."

Sarah recoiled. She had not expected that answer.

"Do you have a crush on your running mate?" the man in red robes asked.

Sarah replayed the last few seconds in her head to make sure she had heard what she thought she had just heard. Mick beamed at her, and though she wanted to shout or yell or demand the interview be terminated, her voice was suddenly out of operation.

"Of course!" Mick said. He winked at Sarah. She wanted to disappear into her chair.

"Let's talk about Earth," the man in red robes said.

Sarah was immensely relieved that the conversation was moving to other topics, but she couldn't help but notice that Mick's air of confidence appeared to have been punctured by the mention of Earth. He glanced at her with what looked like nervousness.

"There are many Astrals who feel that our mother planet has gone astray and the time for reckoning has arrived. Many voters feel it's time to . . . sever ties."

"What did he mean by that?" Sarah interjected. Mick waved at her to stop, but Sarah wasn't in the least bit inclined to stop.

Mick smiled indulgently at Mr. Simon and to the cameras. "You'll love my running mate if you get to know her better."

Sarah slammed her hand on her chair and didn't care how many people on their Astral Tellys saw it.

"Now then," the man in red robes said, "do you want to destroy Earth?"

"What?! Why is he asking you that?" Sarah asked. "Why is that even a question?"

Sarah stared at Mick and he swallowed. It suddenly dawned on her what was happening. She remembered the meeting with the Valkyrians and how Mick promised General Gravy that he would get to destroy the target of his choosing . . . which must have been Earth. He had given away her planet with a handshake, and it had happened right under her nose without her even knowing. She clenched her hands into fists and tried to figure out what she was going to do about it.

"Answer the question please," Mr. Simon said. "Do you want to destroy Earth?"

Mick put his head down and shook it. "No, I don't."

That didn't answer Sarah's question. The issue wasn't whether he *wanted* to destroy Earth, but whether he had already agreed to let it happen. She stood up. "Did you promise the Valkyrians that you would let them destroy Earth when the campaign is over?"

Mick wiped his face and stood up. He smiled, but Sarah could tell his expression was fake. "I sure did," he said. "And ladies and gentlemen of outer space, look closely. I have an Earther representative as my running mate." He smiled his best cocky grin. "Would some say that this is a sign that Earthers see the wisdom in having their planet blown to bits? Thank you, Sarah, for asking that very important question."

Sarah lunged at Mick and tackled him to the floor.

chapter 24

Jacob Wonderbar wasn't exactly sure what eating corndogs had to do with being president of the universe, but if he had to eat more corndogs than Mick Cracken in order to win the first Battle Supreme, that was exactly what he was going to do.

Catalina explained that Father Albert had been a big fan of corndogs before blasting off into space, and consuming them was something of an Astral sport and longstanding tradition. Thus the rules of the first battle, established by the Election Council, were quite simple: Eat as many corndogs as possible in the allotted time without throwing up. Whoever ate the most would win.

Dexter had suggested that Jacob practice eating large quantities of candy in order to stretch his stomach in anticipation of the big event, but Jacob ultimately decided that it was better to go in hungry. Though as a precautionary measure in case of a food overload emergency, he did take Dexter up on his offer to explain proper vomiting technique.

Soon they were interrupted mid-lesson when Catalina told them about Sarah Daisy's assault on her running mate. Jacob and Dexter quickly tuned in to their Tellys and laughed hysterically as they watched Sarah tackle Mick. Dexter recorded a special slow-motion version and narrated the action.

"Okay. Here goes Mick. 'Oh, why, thank you Sarah for asking about how I want to blow up Earth, thank you very much for that.' Now watch Sarah's face. Watch her. Notice the set in her jaw. The whiteness of her knuckles. Decision made: Kill. She jumps out of her chair, runs, and . . . Watch this. BAM! Tackles him to the floor! Down for the count! Let's watch that again." The footage rewound in front of Jacob, then started playing again. Sarah lunged at Mick again. "And . . . BAM! Oh, man."

Jacob laughed, but Catalina was scowling.

"Fifteen percent," she said. "That's how many people plan to vote for us. If you guys think that was a

great moment, think again. Sarah Daisy's popularity among Astrals has skyrocketed after that little attack." She sniffed and tipped up her chin. "I wouldn't be surprised if they staged the whole thing."

Dexter shook his head. "You can't fake that kind of rage."

"Well, either way," Catalina said. "It was not good. Let's hope Jakey here can eat corndogs like his life depends on it."

Jacob swallowed and nodded. He would be a groundbreaking food-eating champion. He would eat until his intestines were made out of corndog batter.

He just hoped he would still be able to look at a corndog after it was all over. It would be a shame to no longer have corndogs in his life.

They arrived at Planet Royale a few hours later and walked proudly into the huge banquet hall, a room with soaring ceilings hung with the various coats of arms of previous Astral dynasties. Reporters were everywhere and shouted questions at Jacob, Dexter, and Catalina, but they ignored them. Boris walked proudly in front of the children, and when one of the reporters moved too close, Boris screeched and pushed him out of the way, looking extremely pleased with himself.

Jacob took his place at a table on a dais piled high with two mountains of corndogs and tried to focus on the task at hand. He wasn't sure if he was more nervous about the upcoming competition or about seeing Sarah again.

There was a commotion at the back of the room as Sarah and Mick walked in. Mick tried to take Sarah's hand, but Sarah pulled her hand away and pushed him.

Sarah and Jacob locked eyes, but then she looked away quickly.

Mick arrived on the dais and sat down next to Jacob.

Jacob said, "May the best man win," and stuck out his hand. Mick stared straight ahead and left him hanging with his hand outstretched.

Jacob wondered if it was against the rules to impale Mick with a corndog stick.

The king stepped forward and the room immediately quieted. "It gives me great pleasure to commence this first Battle Supreme in the race for the presidency. I would like to thank the Election Council for overseeing the rules, and I congratulate these two fine young men on the campaigns they have run thus far. I wish them all the best of luck in the race ahead. The Planet Royale chef has taken great care to produce the finest corndogs humanity has ever eaten, so no doubt your

task will be delicious as well as challenging. You will have twelve septometers to eat as many corndogs as possible, according to my watch." Catalina had previously assured Jacob that twelve septometers was close to two and a half Earther minutes and ignored his rant about how Astral time still didn't make any sense.

The king turned to face Jacob and Mick. "You may begin."

Jacob quickly grabbed a corndog, pulled out the stick, and started chomping as fast as he could. The king was right. It was a fantastically delicious corndog, even better than the one he once had at Disneyland, previously the gold standard in corndog culinary excellence. But he didn't have time to focus on the flavor. He needed to cram them down his gullet as fast as possible.

It wasn't until after he finished his fourth corndog that Jacob noticed that Mick hadn't started eating. He hadn't even touched one of the corndogs. He was just sitting there smiling at the crowd.

"What are you doing?" Jacob asked between bites.

Mick looked at Jacob as if he had just noticed he was there. He patted Jacob on the back with mock concern and whispered, "I poisoned your corndogs."

Jacob stopped chewing for a second and swallowed. "You're lying."

Mick kept on smiling. "The first symptom will be a tightening feeling in your stomach. Then you'll start to feel warm in the face. And eventually you will throw up harder than you have ever thrown up in your life and you'll be disqualified. I have this one in the bag."

Jacob was indeed feeling a tightening in his stomach, but it could have been a result of eating a corndog and a half in less than twenty seconds. He kept on eating, but he couldn't help but notice that his face was starting to feel a little warm. He slowed down his pace. At that precise moment, Mick grabbed a corndog and ate it in an incredible blur of chomps and swallows.

Jacob began to feel even more nauseated as he started chomping on his seventh corndog, and Mick was steadily gaining on him. As the cheering in the dining hall reached a fever pitch, Jacob felt another campaign event slipping away. Mick had psyched him out yet again, and Jacob felt so unsure of himself. It was an unfamiliar and horrible feeling. Back on Earth he had outlasted substitutes, beat up the MacKenzie twins two-on-one, pulled more pranks than anyone he knew. He had flown to outer space and back and broken the universe and lived to tell the tale. But no matter how good he tried to be in the campaign, nothing seemed to be working.

And then it hit him. He had been trying so hard to be good that somewhere along the way he had stopped being Jacob Wonderbar.

"Two septometers left," the king shouted above the ruckus.

Jacob smiled at Mick, who seemed to sense that something important was about to happen. And then Jacob sneezed all over Mick's corndogs. Mick finished the corndog he was eating and stared at his pile with his jaw hanging open.

Mick quickly recovered and seemed to be moving his mouth around in an attempt to collect saliva to spit on Jacob's corndogs. But Jacob quickly grabbed two and shielded them from Mick. He chomped and chomped as quickly as he could, while Mick tried to eat his snot-covered ones gingerly, his eyes watering.

"Five . . . four . . . three . . ." the king chanted.

Jacob finished the last few bites of his corndog.

"Two . . . one . . ."

He swallowed and held up his thirteenth stick.

"Time!" the king shouted.

Jacob looked over at Mick. He'd only eaten twelve.

Jacob Wonderbar was back.

chapter 25

As soon as the first Battle Supreme was over, Sarah Daisy slipped out of the banquet hall and back aboard Mick Jr. before anyone noticed she was gone. She smiled a little when she pictured the look on Mick's face when Jacob sneezed all over his corndogs, and she was proud of Jake for finally showing the universe what he was made of. But she couldn't talk to him or the reporters or anyone else. She needed some time to think.

"What are *you* doing here?" Mick Jr. sneered when she stepped on board.

"Leave me alone," she said.

"I'm going to tell master that you're here."

She kicked a wall, even if it wouldn't hurt Mick Jr.

since he couldn't feel pain. "If you tell him I'm here I'll program you to fly straight into a star before anyone even knows you're missing."

She waited a few seconds for a response, and Mick Jr. finally said, "You're just mad because I'm such an amazing spaceship."

Sarah grabbed her own hair and pulled it. She didn't have time to argue with a conceited bucket of plastic and gears.

She plopped down on her lavender comforter and tried to decide what she should do. She had been so focused on stopping Jacob Wonderbar from winning the election so that they could go home, she hadn't even realized that Mick was helping with a plot to destroy her planet. Even if she suspected that Mick wouldn't have the heart to blow up Earth while she was on it, she had seen enough of the crazy Valkyrians to know that they would jump at the opportunity. Most Astrals seemed to think that Earth was just a backward, war-torn, polluted place. It was easy to blow up a planet when you didn't stop to think that there were good people living there.

Still, the election had given her an opportunity to show Astrals that Earthers weren't so bad after all, and her fight with Mick had improved her poll numbers.

She was a little flattered that after she attacked Mick the Astrals had started to think she was one of them.

It wasn't as if Mick made the promise to the Valkyrians on Planet Veritas. Maybe the pledge to let them blow up Earth was one of the many promises he intended to break. Maybe the best thing she could do would be to become so popular herself that the idea of blowing up Earth would become unthinkable.

Her Telly announced, "Call from Jacob Wonderbar."

She stared at the Telly and thought about talking to Jacob, but she didn't know what she would say. She just wasn't ready. "Ignore," she said.

She heard footsteps outside her room, and she jumped up and found Mick in the hallway. She could tell he was furious about losing.

"Hey," he said quietly. "Please . . . Don't say the word corn . . ." He gagged and steadied himself and said, "Well, you know. That word. Ever again."

Sarah crossed her arms. "We need to talk."

He shrugged and waited for her to say something. He was scowling and clearly did not want to talk to her, but she at least preferred a surly expression to his normal conceited cockiness.

"I want to know if you're really planning on letting the Valkyrians blow up Earth."

Mick rubbed his temples and sighed. "We need to start planning your introduction rally. Earth is the least of our worries right now."

"It's not the least of *my* worries! Has it ever occurred to you that my parents and my sisters and my friends are on that planet?"

"Yes," Mick snapped. "I know. Your family and your friends and everything and everyone you care about in the universe are on Earth. I get it."

Sarah was a bit taken aback by Mick's heated tone. "Well, not *everyone* I care about," she said.

Mick leaned against the wall and rubbed his nose. "All I've ever wanted since I was little was to be president. Not king. President. I wanted to earn it. I didn't want it handed to me and for everyone to just think I was in charge because of who my dad was. And I promised myself I would do whatever it takes to get it." He gave her a pointed look. "*Whatever* it takes. Including convincing my dad to give up his throne. It's the right thing for everyone, and I'm going to be a great president."

Sarah didn't say anything. She remembered how vehement Mick had been about democracy when

they had been captured by the royal guards on her last trip to space, but at the time he seemed far more concerned with being the universe's greatest space pirate than becoming the future president of every-thing.

He leaned in to look at her straight in the eye. "But look. I appreciate you helping me out on this cam-paign. I couldn't do this without you. If I win I'll stop the Valkyrians from destroying Earth. I promise. Earth will be fine."

Sarah nodded and gave him a sweet smile and said, "Thanks, Mick. I trust you."

Mick stumbled away toward his stateroom holding his stomach.

Sarah most certainly did not trust him. She was quite sure he was lying about saving Earth. But in that moment she realized that she would have a bet-ter chance of stopping the Valkyrians if she were vice president. Earth needed someone influential on the inside of the Astral government. Even if that meant she would have to stay in space after all, she knew she had to do it to protect her planet.

If she stayed on the campaign, she was giving Earth a sure chance of survival. If Jacob won the election, he could save Earth and get rid of the Valkyrians. And if Mick won, Sarah could do her best to stop them as Mick's vice president.

Either way, she knew she couldn't quit Mick's campaign.

chapter 26

You look amazing, champ. Exquisite! I just need you to hold that position for two beats."

Jacob was holding hands with a woman who looked somewhat but not exactly like his mother on a set that looked somewhat but not exactly like his house on a planet that was absolutely nothing like any place he had ever been. His "mother" was a bit younger than his real mom and her skin was lighter, and Jacob found the differences somewhat offensive. Catalina had assured him she was the closest approximation they could find on short notice.

A director in dark black sunglasses directed his every move and facial expression. Jacob was growing very tired of trying to act out his everyday life.

Also, he was reasonably sure he had seen the Astral actress on a daytime soap opera he had watched one day when he was home from school.

It had been Catalina's idea to humanize Jacob by filming a campaign commercial that would portray him as a normal, average, and unthreatening kid from Earth, but nothing about arriving at Planet Cut! Cut! or pretending that the actress was his mom felt normal. In fact, the whole thing was quite bizarre and uncomfortable.

"Hi," Jacob said to the camera, reciting the lines that Catalina had written for him. "I'm Jacob Wonderbar, just a normal kid from Earth. This is my mom. She's an Earther too. You might be surprised that she doesn't make me live in a basement and eat mice for dinner. Nope. She wants what's best for me, and hopes that someday I'll grow up and keep her entertained in her twilight years, just like any other mom."

Jacob thought the lines were stupid, but Catalina insisted they would help him with the Astral mother demographic.

"Great, champ!" the director shouted. "Now, just look at your mom, and I want you to look very, very sad. Like, so crazy sad as if your dog flew away mixed with your grandmother dying mixed with seeing the last scene of *Astral Tuesday*. Go with that! Work it!"

"Hey," Jacob whispered to the actress as he tried to look sad. "Have you been to Earth?"

"Don't lose the feeling!" the director shouted. "I mean, Jacob darling, you've got to own this scene. Own it! Sad, champ. Look very sad."

"Many times," the woman whispered. "You know, many of the people you see in Hollywood are Astrals . . ."

Jacob let go of her hand in surprise and forgot about looking sad. "How many Astrals are on—"

The director shoved over his cloth director's chair and yelled, "Cut! Cut! You people . . . Ugh! The magic is gone. I can't work under these conditions. EVERYONE TAKE FIVE!" The director wandered off muttering to himself and Jacob thought he heard him sobbing when he reached his trailer.

Catalina stepped over, clapping. "Jakey, this is great!"

There were many words that Jacob would have used to describe the experience of filming the campaign commercial, and *great* was not one of them.

"Just one more scene to go," she said. "We want to dramatize what happened with your dad leaving you behind and—"

"How do you know about my dad?" Jacob said, the blood suddenly rushing through his ears. He had

never once spoken to Catalina about his father, and in fact he hardly ever even talked to Sarah and Dexter about it. They at least had the common sense and decency to broach the topic very lightly and carefully so that whenever Jacob didn't want to talk about it he didn't have to, and they certainly would have known without asking that he wouldn't want the whole thing paraded around in front of Astrals as a way of getting a few more votes. He looked around at the crew members fussing with props in the house and touching up the paint. He loathed the idea of talking about his father in front of them.

"Oh," Catalina said. "Oh, Jakey, well . . . You do remember that I was there with you aboard Praiseworthy last time you were in space when you found the pipe and wanted to go looking for your dad and you had that big fight with Sarah and Dex? I haven't been *investigating* you or anything. I just thought it was a dramatic moment that—"

"What do you know about it?" he said, trying not to yell.

Catalina's face went white, and she looked as if she couldn't decide whether to smile or cry. "Nothing, Jacob. Nothing. I just thought . . . You know, not everyone has two parents, and that's something that many Astrals can relate to. It Astralizes you."

In a distant region of his brain he realized that he had never heard Catalina mention her mother and hadn't really thought about the fact that there wasn't a queen of the universe. But he was too mad about the commercial and the mention of his dad to calm down. That actress was not his mom and didn't even look like his mom. Catalina was always trying to make things fine by faking everything.

"Where's Dexter?" Jacob asked. He knew that Dexter would understand.

Catalina wiped a fleck of mascara out of her eyelash. "He's taking care of the monkeys."

Jacob started walking away, but Catalina jumped in front of him.

"Jacob," Catalina said quietly. "I'm sorry if I made you upset. I . . . I care about you. I really, really do. You know that, right?"

Jacob stared at her a moment and thought about the wrinkled postcard sitting on his shelf back on Earth. "Have you ever heard of a place called Dakota, Arizona?"

Catalina blinked. "What? I . . ."

"Have you ever heard of a place called Dakota, Arizona?!"

"No!" she said quickly. "No, I haven't. Is that where you're from?"

169

Jacob shook his head and kept walking. He knew he shouldn't be so frustrated with Catalina, that she was just trying to help, and she had done her best to jump-start the campaign. He also knew that she really did like him, maybe too much. But she just didn't understand him. He didn't want to fake being an Astral, even if it worked.

It was time for him to be himself. And it was time to plan something bigger than a campaign commercial. To do something really spectacular.

"I'll be in my trailer," he said, and he walked away.

He waited for Catalina to challenge him, but she let him go.

Sarah knew from the poll numbers that she was growing popular among Astrals, but it wasn't until she looked out at the hundreds of thousands of people who had gathered on Planet Stupendia that she had any idea exactly what those numbers meant in real life. There was a big difference between seeing on her Telly that 74 percent of Astrals liked her versus actually seeing a huge, cheering, excited mob that had come out in droves just to hear her speak.

After noticing the huge spike in her popularity numbers, it had been Sarah's idea to throw a big introductory event where she could speak to Astrals in order to demonstrate her popularity and hopefully win over the remaining skeptics. Mick had suggested they hold it on Stupendia, the most beautiful of the

Astral planets, which had been reserved entirely for hiking enthusiasts and nature lovers. It featured spectacular sunsets every six Earth hours, followed by majestic auroras in the nighttime sky. Mick figured it would give the best visuals.

Sarah had taken side trips to the Grand Canyon and Yosemite during some of the college visits that her parents organized every summer, but those natural wonders paled in comparison to the physical beauty of Stupendia. The area they had reserved for the adoring crowds was in a valley surrounded by majestic snow-capped peaks, and behind Sarah was a green glacial lake that looked like it stretched on into infinity. The sky was perfectly blue and she was sure she'd never breathed such pure, unpolluted air. She figured half the people tuning in on their Tellys would be doing so just to experience the wonderful views.

The crowd cheered as Mick stepped to the podium to give her a brief introduction. She could barely listen to him, she was so nervous. She had never given a speech before, let alone before hundreds of thousands of people and millions around the universe watching on their Tellys. Her ears pricked up when she thought she heard Mick say she was working on her anger management issues, but she was still too distracted to really listen.

Finally, she heard Mick say, "And now, allow me to introduce my running mate, someone who reports to me, and who it was my idea to choose . . . Sarah Daisy."

The crowd gave a deafening roar. Sarah couldn't help but note that she had received a louder ovation than Mick. She wondered if he noticed.

When the cheering finally died down several minutes later, she cleared her throat and said "Hi," into the microphone. The crowd erupted in cheers again and Sarah had to wait another couple of minutes for them to give her another standing ovation.

"Your support means a lot to me!" Sarah Daisy said as the cheering finally ebbed.

Sarah had given her speech a great deal of thought and had a feeling she knew exactly what to say. She had even curled her hair with swoops and swirls in what she hoped was a particularly Astral style.

She gave her voice a folksy inflection. "When I was growing up, why, I was too poor to go to space. I looked up the stars and I said to my daddy, 'Golly, I sure hope I can go up there one day.' I was just a little Earther girl with a big dream."

Sarah didn't like to call herself an Earther, but she knew that was what the Astrals wanted.

"And then one day a spaceship arrived, and it

changed my life forever." She leaned into the microphone. "But *not* in the way I expected."

She paused for dramatic effect. She sensed things were going well.

"What I didn't know at the time was that there was an incredible civilization out in space. So much more advanced than us silly little Earthers. You have so much to teach us. And so much love to give."

The crowd roared at the mention of love, and over the din she heard many Astrals shout, "We love you, Sarah!" She waved at the crowd for silence.

"But gosh darn it, you don't want to listen to me and this boring speech, do you? You don't need to hear me go on for hours. I'm going to . . ."

This was the key moment in the speech. She knew she couldn't wow them solely with her words. They needed something more exciting than that.

She ran to the side of the stage, hopped on a flying motorcycle, revved it loudly, and the crowd gasped in excitement when she sailed over them. They cheered in surprise and jumped up and down. She threw out candy as she flew over, and then pressed a button and her motorcycle lit up with lights.

She completed her tour over the crowd and soared back to the stage, relieved that a day of flying motorcycle practice had been sufficient to prevent her from crashing into the side of a mountain.

She hopped off the motorcycle and walked back to the stage as the crowd chanted her name. She signaled for silence, and waited until the entire crowd was completely hushed. Then she whispered, "Thank you, Astrals. I love you."

The crowd let out its most deafen-

ing cheer. She waved and waved and smiled until her cheeks hurt.

She knew she had nailed it. They loved her. There was no way they would want to destroy Earth if she were living on it, and she might have just ensured that she would be the future vice president of the universe. She beamed at Mick, but he didn't smile back.

She didn't care if he was jealous.

chapter 28

Amid the tremendous amount of spaceship traffic entering Stupendia for the Sarah Daisy rally, no one seemed to notice a newly disguised Praiseworthy slip into the atmosphere. Jacob and Dexter had personally painted Praiseworthy black and taken down the flags and streamers for this important secret mission. Praiseworthy stayed as far away from other ships as possible, and Jacob made sure all incoming communications traffic was jammed.

"Master Wonderbar, this is terrifically exciting!" Praiseworthy shouted. "I feel I am a buccaneer ship all over again. Tally ho, dare I say!"

As they flew over the valley where the rally was being held, Jacob was stunned by the number of Astrals who had turned out to see Sarah Daisy. They stretched across the entire meadow, and he wasn't sure he had ever seen so many people in one place. Many people held banners and posters with Sarah's face. He knew she had become popular, but it was still awe-inspiring to see how excited the Astrals were to see her in person.

Catalina and Dexter emerged from their state-rooms wearing their disguises, dressed in black from head to toe. Jacob was already dressed and ready to go, and pulled on a black backpack that held their essential supplies.

"Ready?"

"Ready." They nodded.

Jacob was surprised that Dexter was not having a mild-to-severe panic attack, which was his usual mental state prior to pulling a prank. He seemed uncharacteristically giddy, and Jacob couldn't tell if he was excited about facing certain danger or if he was completely terrified.

They slipped out into the Stupendia wilderness. The planet's orange sun had set, and the twilight was bright enough that they could see where they were going, but was just dark enough that they could easily disguise themselves among the trees. Sarah's voice echoed around the surrounding mountains, punctuated occasionally by cheering Astrals.

They ran along a small stream toward the massive lake behind Sarah's rally platform. Dexter tripped a few times over rocks and boulders, but managed to keep up. Catalina grabbed Jacob's hand for balance a few more times than he thought was probably necessary.

Finally they reached the shore of the lake. Jacob peered around until he spotted a black mass in a clearing between them and the rally platform.

"Jackpot," he whispered.

He signaled Catalina and Dexter to follow him, and they crept along until they had reached a sleek black spaceship sitting completely alone and unguarded in a small clearing. Jacob couldn't believe that Mick Cracken had left his ship defenseless.

Jacob set down the pack and divvied up its contents. Catalina and Dexter quietly took their supplies and slunk off into the forest. Jacob heard another wild cheer and he had a feeling the speech was nearing its end. Catalina and Dexter needed to hurry to time everything just right.

He took out a can of spray paint and walked over to Mick Jr. The ship's hull gleamed even in the dim light, and Jacob almost felt bad about what he was about to do.

Almost.

Jacob started spraying. He worked quickly, moved over a bit, added a few more letters. He finished off with one long underline.

He stepped back and admired his handiwork. It was beautiful. The words "WONDERBAR RULES!" were painted in bright orange along the entire length of the ship. He only wished he could see the expression on Mick's face when he saw it.

Jacob heard the loudest cheer yet, and when the applause kept going and going, he knew the speech was finished. He held his breath, waiting for Dexter and Catalina to complete their mission.

He heard a loud explosion. He laughed and pumped his fist and started running toward the sound.

As he ran, he looked up into the sky as gigantic fireworks lit up the valley with the words "CRACKEN STINKS!" A hush fell over the Astrals.

Jacob reached into his pocket and quickly pulled on his face mask, but he still caught a whiff of the horrible rotten egg stink bomb that lent the proper accompaniment to their message. He heard a second explosion and the sky lit up again, this time with

"WONDERBAR FOR PRESIDENT!"

He reached the small clearing where Dexter and Catalina had set off the fireworks and they all high-fived. Dexter gave Jacob an awkward chest bump.

"That was awesome!" Dexter yelled.

"Shh!" Jacob whispered. "Come on, we need to get back to Praiseworthy."

Dexter shook his head. "No. I want to chase this feeling. One more prank."

Jacob's heart raced. They needed to get back to Praiseworthy and blast off before they were caught by some of Mick's Planet Valkyrie goons.

"Dexter, no. We—"

Jacob was too late. Dexter had already run off in the direction of Mick Jr.

"Dexter!" he whispered after him, but Dexter kept going.

He kicked a rock and whispered to Catalina, "Get back to the ship. I'll go get Dexter and—"

Jacob heard a rustling sound. He turned in time to see Rufus bounding through the clearing. He screeched at Jacob and charged off in Dexter's direction.

"Oh no," Jacob said.

He started running after Rufus. Jacob could hear voices growing closer and knew that Mick's men were probably closing in.

He had almost reached the clearing and still hadn't seen any sign of Dexter when Jacob suddenly tripped and went sprawling onto the ground. Whatever had tripped him was soft and almost felt . . . human.

"Sorry," Dexter whispered. He pressed his face back into the ground.

Jacob glanced around to see if anyone had spotted them. They were safe for now.

"What are you doing?" Jacob asked.

"I changed my mind," Dexter whispered. "Being brave is scary."

They heard a monkey's screech and Rufus swung

among the branches above them before scrambling down a tree and into the clearing toward Mick's ship.

"Rufus, no!" Dexter whispered.

"Dexter, get him back!" Jacob whispered.

"I can't," Dexter said.

Rufus scrambled over to the ship and pounded on its side, creating a huge echoing racket. Jacob prepared to run away. He couldn't risk his entire campaign to save a monkey.

Rufus bounded over to the silver "Mick Jr." signature plate and stared at it for a moment. He reached out and touched the silver longingly with his fingers. Then, with a mighty heave, he pulled the plate straight off of the ship. He jumped up and down in triumph and ran over to Jacob and Dexter with his trophy.

Jacob laughed. "Nice one, Rufus!"

Just as he was about to turn to run away, Jacob saw Mick Cracken. He had reached the clearing. Mick stared at his defaced ship for a few seconds with his hands on his hips. Then he whipped his head around and looked into the forest. He spotted Jacob and they locked eyes.

Mick looked completely, utterly furious.

But Jacob knew he was impressed.

chapter 29

By the time the second Battle Supreme arrived, eleven Earth days into the election, the Wonderbar and Cracken campaigns had settled into a virtual tie in the polls. Sarah was still wildly popular after her speech to the Astrals, but Jacob's prank had been viewed as a stroke of genius, and Sarah and Mick were clinging to the smallest of leads going into the final week of the campaign.

Sarah knew she had to beat Catalina in the vice presidential battle in order to give her campaign an edge. Not that she needed extra motivation to beat Princess Twinkle Toes at anything.

The ballroom on Planet Royale hushed as the event was about to begin. Sarah and Catalina were sitting in large chairs on the dais. Sarah looked out and spotted the king, his hands clasped in contemplation. She wondered what he was thinking of all of this.

Sarah cleared her throat and said to Catalina, "You are the film that forms on the walls of a shower after several weeks of use."

It wasn't her best insult, but she was just warming up. The Election Council seemed mildly impressed and gave her a 6.5. The Cracken/Daisy supporters clapped politely in response, and a few jeered at the judges for not sufficiently rewarding the disgusting-ness of shower film.

The purpose of the second Battle Supreme was to show Astrals who would be the very best vice president by way of an insult contest. Mick had explained to Sarah that since the president couldn't very well go around tell-ing people off and still seem presidential, it would be up to the vice president to get down in the muck and insult the people who needed insulting, mock the people who needed mocking, and possibly throw a nice solid temper tantrum every now and then for good measure. Sarah could hardly contain her glee at the thought of spending an afternoon criticizing Princess Catalina.

Princess Catalina batted her eyelashes and leaned in toward Sarah. "Your clothes are at least three sea-sons out of style," she said, barely adding any disdain in her voice.

Sarah grimaced and scanned the crowd until she found Jacob Wonderbar, who ran a hand through his hair and appeared thoroughly disappointed with Princess Catalina's attempt at an insult. The Election Council gave her a 3.

Sarah leaned in for her next attempt. "I would rather step in gum on a dirty street, peel it off my shoe, place it in my mouth, chew, and swallow than spend one minute in the same room with you."

The crowd "Oohed" appreciatively. Sarah was particularly fond of that insult because it was completely true. The Election Council gave her an 8.

Princess Catalina punched Sarah in the arm playfully. "Oh Sarah, you're my funniest friend," she said.

The Election Council looked at each other in confusion before giving her a 0.5. Sarah wasn't even sure where the half of a point came from.

"Um," Sarah said, trying to regain her footing. It was not easy insulting someone who wasn't putting up a fight. "Um. You're . . . I mean . . . You smell like a red-butted baboon who just . . ." Catalina was beaming innocently at Sarah, and she found it wildly unnerving. "Who just took a bath in a steaming pile of baby diapers."

The council awarded Sarah a 6, which she attributed to her imperfect delivery.

Catalina smiled. "You're almost but not quite as pretty as me."

Sarah frowned as the council gave Catalina a 3. Sarah had no idea what Catalina was up to, but Sarah was on the verge of winning the second Battle Supreme, and there was no stopping her now. No one

would doubt that she would be the better vice president. She could insult with the best of them, which perfectly complemented her "aw shucks" Earther girl routine. In just over a week she had gone from anonymous Earth kid and Jacob Wonderbar afterthought to one of the most popular people in the entire universe. She was going to save her planet and make the universe a better place. She looked out at Mick, who was smiling faintly and pumping his fist slowly in appreciation of her talents.

Sarah darted her eyes at Catalina and readied her finest salvo. "You're so ugly, when you tried to kiss a frog to turn him into a prince he said, 'Ugh! No thanks, I'd rather be a frog.'"

There was a roaring ovation, and Sarah raised her hands in glee when she saw her score: 9.5.

Princess Catalina kept beaming. Technically she had one last insult remaining, but there was no way she could catch up to Sarah. Catalina smiled and said, "Jacob Wonderbar would rather spend time with me than a silly little Earther girl like you. And that's why he dumped you."

Sarah's jaw clenched, and she felt her face grow very warm. "At least I'm not a conceited alien!" she snapped. After a few gasps and shrieks, the room fell completely, uncomfortably silent. Sarah looked around

in confusion. Mick had crouched down on the ground and was covering his eyes in agony. People looked at her as if she had just sprouted a second head.

"What?" Sarah asked.

For the briefest, tiniest of moments, Sarah saw a look pass across Princess Catalina's face that showed unbridled triumph at what Sarah had just said, her joy plain and unmistakable. And in that split second Sarah knew she had been suckered. She remembered that shocked look on Catalina's face when she had called her an alien on Planet Headline and she suddenly realized that Catalina must have planned this moment all along.

Princess Catalina's face contorted into a mask of pain and anguish. She summoned tears, pressed her face into her hands, and wailed, "How dare you, Sarah Daisy?"

The uncomfortable silence in the ballroom stretched on. Princess Catalina peeled her hands from her face, and Sarah could tell she was trying not to smile.

"How *dare* you."

chapter 30

This is amazing! This is amazing! This is amazing!" Catalina skipped around Praiseworthy, tossing pillows into the air and dancing. She ran over to Jacob and hugged him and didn't even seem to care that he bristled and didn't hug her back. "Did you hear what she called me? It's amazing!"

Jacob scratched his chin and tried to make sense of what was happening. "I mean . . . I heard her call you a conceited alien."

"Oh dearest me, Master Wonderbar!" Praiseworthy gasped. "I wish you wouldn't use such filthy language aboard my ship."

Catalina pranced over to Jacob and threw a jeweled necklace around his neck. "The A-word is the gravest insult you can ever call an Astral. We *hate* that word.

We're people, not al . . . well, you know. And now everyone is going to be so upset with Sarah for calling me that, we have the election in the bag. Jakey, isn't this great?"

Jacob took off the necklace and sat down in the captain's chair. He was feeling very tired, and even though the election was just four Earth days away, it felt like an eternity. They had been in space for almost two weeks, and he missed his mom and wanted to sleep in his own bed. Sunday Family Bonding Night and his mom's sketchy cooking didn't even seem like such a bad thing, and he wished he could just call her and say hello and chat for a little while.

Dexter walked into the cockpit, holding Rufus by the hand. From the ruckus in the rear of the ship, it sounded like the monkeys were thoroughly enjoying the Planet Royale chef's latest banana creation.

"What's the deal with all this 'alien' stuff?" Dexter asked.

"Master Goldstein!" Praiseworthy exclaimed. "You too?! Galloping grasshoppers, this ship might as well be a saloon."

"This 'A' stuff is only the best thing that has ever happened to our campaign!" Catalina said. "This will go down as one of the greatest gaffes in history!"

Jacob looked at Dexter and shook his head in confu-

sion. Astrals had long since stopped making sense to him.

"But you're not even upset," Jacob said. "How could this be so bad if she didn't even make you angry? It's not like she knew what that word meant."

Catalina gave Jacob a very patient smile. "Jakey, don't you see? I'm going to go on all the interviews on ANN and look upset and cry and talk about what a horrible insult this is. I might even demand an apology." She had a dreamy smile, but then seemed to change her mind and shook her head. "No. First I'll talk about how upset I am and how I want the whole thing to just blow over for the good of Earther/Astral relations. Then when things start to die down I'll demand an apology. Then if she apologizes I'll say her apology isn't good enough and that I just feel so bad for my fellow Astrals for having to endure such a horrible insult. Because she didn't just upset me, she upset *all* Astrals."

Jacob stared at Catalina incredulously. "But you're not upset!"

Catalina put her hands on her hips. "Jacob Wonderbar, I hardly see how that is relevant. This was a gift! Sarah Daisy just handed us the election in a nice, sweet little filthy-worded box. Here's what you need to do. You need to denounce her and stand firm to show that not all Earthers are Astral-haters."

"I'm not going to denounce her! You know she didn't mean it that way. How was she supposed to know that the worst word you can say in outer space is 'alien'?"

"Oh!" Praiseworthy exclaimed. "Oh, I'm feeling faint."

Catalina's eyes narrowed. Jacob glanced quickly at Dexter, who sat straight up, alarmed that Catalina was at last showing an emotion that resembled anger.

"Well, Jacob Wonderbar," she muttered through clenched teeth. "And here I thought you wanted to *win* this election."

"I do!"

"Do you? Do you, Jacob?" she shrieked. "Or are your feelings for your blondie Earther girl going to stand in the way of us winning? *Us*, Jacob? You and me?"

Jacob saw that tears were forming in Catalina's eyes, and a part of him was actually glad that she was finally standing up for herself and being honest about her feelings.

But the more he thought about it, the more he knew he was right.

The truth was that he *did* care more about Sarah Daisy than winning the election. He couldn't bring himself to betray her, no matter how important it was and how much he had put into the election. Catalina knew Sarah didn't mean it, Catalina wasn't really hurt by it, and Jacob wasn't going to pretend any differently. He was going to win by doing things his own way.

"You can say what you want," Jacob said. "You can do all the interviews you want and cry all you want and drag her through the mud. But I want no part of this alien business."

"Master Wonderbar!" Praiseworthy exclaimed.

"Sorry! I won't say it again."

"No, not that. We're under attack!"

chapter 31

Sarah stared at the wreckage of her political career, which came to her in the form of a video chart on board Mick Jr.

Five percent. Only five percent of Astrals still liked her. Only five percent of Astrals believed she wasn't a horrible person just because she said a word that she had no idea was considered a grave insult in outer space. Never mind that she had been engaged in an *insult* competition at the time she said it. No. Somehow she had gone too far. One word was enough to upend everything she had worked so hard to achieve. No one stopped to think that maybe she hadn't meant it that way or that maybe she just didn't know any better or that maybe she was still the same person they had liked a lot right up until that moment and that nothing had really changed.

And they had really liked her! She thought back to standing in front of a cheering mob on Stupendia and feeling the energy of the crowd and seeing that love. She wanted it back, so unbelievably badly.

More importantly, she had let her entire planet down. The Astrals already thought Earth was dangerous and hostile, and she had confirmed their worst fears. She had been so close to showing them that Earthers were great too.

But it was all gone. All because of one word.

Mick came up alongside her and stared at the numbers, holding his chin in his hand.

"Mick," Sarah said. "You know I didn't mean anything by that . . . that word . . ."

Mick didn't look at her, but nodded faintly. "I know."

"It was just a word! How was I supposed to know it would make everyone so upset?"

"You couldn't have," he said quietly.

She had done so much for his campaign and had technically won the second Battle Supreme. If she hadn't let that stupid princess get to her, she could have just gone on her way and basked in a big victory.

Instead her entire reputation in outer space was in tatters. She pulled out her Telly and thought about turning on ANN to see what they were saying about her, but she wasn't sure if she could bear it.

She looked at Mick and she felt so desperate for him to reassure her that it was going to be fine and that people would see the real her again, and not some cartoon of a person who hates Astrals and uses bad words.

"Mick, you really know I don't hate Astrals, right? I didn't mean it . . ." Her nerves felt so frayed, she was on the verge of tears.

Mick stared at her for a moment with a grim expression. "Look. It's going to be fine. We're going to have a press conference, and I'm going to stand beside you. Okay? This will all blow over. I still plan on winning this election."

Sarah nodded without saying anything. She knew it would be fine eventually. Even when she did horrible things to her sister The Brat and felt badly about it afterward, eventually they forgave each other and moved on. Bad times always felt like they'd never end, but after enough time passes, they finally do. They always do. She would apologize sincerely, and they'd all move on. It would be fine.

"Okay." Sarah nodded. "I think that's a good idea."

Mick took out his Telly and showed it to Sarah. "You ready?"

Sarah felt her knees go weak, but she knew she could get through it. "Yes, I'm ready."

Mick accepted an incoming conference call on his Telly and suddenly there were reporters all around them. "Mr. Cracken! Ms. Daisy!" they shouted in a jumble.

Mick held up his hand for calm. Eventually the reporters stopped shouting, and he began to speak.

"This has been a difficult time for our campaign, as I'm sure you know. I promised the world a dramatic campaign, but this isn't quite the drama we expected."

Sarah's heart sank at Mick's beginning. She hadn't intended to cause any drama at all. She just wanted people to like her.

Mick continued, "My running mate is a good person. A very good person. She has taught me a lot about how to run a good campaign, and I think it's safe to say that this campaign wouldn't have been as successful without her. She tells me that she did not know that the A-word is a grave insult to Astrals, and I believe her. Sarah Daisy would never do anything to hurt this campaign or the Astrals she cares so much about. She wants to do what's best for the Mick Cracken campaign and for the Astral nation as a whole."

Sarah blinked through tears and tried to smile at Mick. She was immensely grateful to hear those words.

"And that is why she will be leaving the Mick Cracken campaign, effective immediately. She is no longer my running mate. That is all."

Sarah's jaw dropped. "What?!" she shrieked. The reporters all started shouting questions simultaneously, and there was a great deal of commotion.

Mick said, "Sarah, don't . . ."

"You said you'd defend me!"

Mick shook his head. He whispered, "I said I'd stand beside you. And, well, technically we are standing beside each other."

Sarah tried to say something but couldn't find the words.

"You're out," Mick said.

chapter 32

Jacob scanned the monitors and saw the Valkyrians gaining on Praiseworthy with their three eagle-shaped ships. They hadn't fired any shots . . . yet.

He gave Catalina, Dexter, and Rufus a grim smile to help them be brave. Rufus chirped with worry.

"Praiseworthy, can you outrun them?" Jacob asked.

"Master Wonderbar, if I did not already think so highly of you, I might be offended by that question. I assure you it will not be a problem."

Space blurred as Praiseworthy shifted into high gear, and Jacob breathed a sigh of relief. The Valkyrians should have known better than to try and stop Praiseworthy, one of the fastest ships in the universe.

A light on the console flashed red. "Praiseworthy, what's that light?" Jacob asked.

Praiseworthy gasped. "How dare they! They're shooting me with a . . ."

The ship shook with a mighty heave, and sparks flew from the console. "What happened?" Dexter asked.

Praiseworthy came to a stop, and then they started speeding backward, directly toward the Valkyrians.

"Stop! Praiseworthy, stop!" Jacob shouted.

"Praiseworthy!" Catalina said. "What are you doing?"

"Bolt backward a with me shot they!" Praiseworthy shouted.

The children looked around at one another frantically. "What?!" Catalina asked.

"Bolt backward! Me shot they!" Praiseworthy shouted.

"That doesn't make any sense!" Catalina cried. "You shot them with what?"

Jacob checked the monitors, and the Valkyrians were dangerously close now that Praiseworthy was heading in reverse. It dawned on him what was happening. "Backward bolt! Praiseworthy's talking backward, they shot him with a backward bolt! It's making him go backward!"

"Happened what exactly that's! Wonderbar Master you thank!" Praiseworthy shouted.

"What are we going to do?" Catalina asked.

Jacob stared at the console. He knew what he had to do. If Praiseworthy was out of commission, he had to fly the ship. Someone had to get them going in the right direction.

Only the last time he took control of a ship, he ended up breaking the universe in a giant space kapow. His heart pounded in his chest, but he knew he had to overcome his fears and fly the ship.

He felt a hand on his shoulder. "You can do this," Dexter said. "I know you can."

He felt another hand on his other shoulder. Rufus screeched in his ear.

Jacob slammed the manual override button and took the wheel. He shoved it forward and the ship creaked to a stop before it started heading in the right direction again. He swung back and forth in erratic arcs just in case the Valkyrians were thinking of hitting them with a bolt that made Praiseworthy even crazier.

"Haw-yee! Wonderbar Master flying good very!" Praiseworthy said.

Jacob was getting used to the controls, and he

started to relax. He could do this. He wasn't going to destroy the universe.

A voice filled the cockpit. "You might as well surrender," Patrick Gravy said. "We'll get you soon enough."

Jacob yelled, "Praiseworthy, tell them they won't catch me in a million years, and when I'm president they're going to pay for this!"

"To happy be would I!" Praiseworthy exclaimed.

Jacob wasn't feeling as confident as he sounded. The Valkyrians were proving relentless, and they would clearly do anything to get him. He wasn't sure how long he could outlast a crazy group of highly trained commandos, and Mick was probably even more motivated to stop him now that Jacob was gaining on him in the polls. They needed to get somewhere they could hide out.

"Catalina, check the maps and find out where we are," Jacob said.

A bright gold beam shot out in front of the cockpit window. "That was close!" Dexter yelled. Jacob swung hard to the right.

"Oh!" Catalina said. "We're close to Planet Blueprint. Jacob, head in a forty-five-degree angle at full throttle."

Jacob did as he was told. Maybe they could get help. "What's Planet Blueprint?" he asked.

"It's where all the construction workers live," Catalina said.

Everything was silent for a moment, until Dexter sighed loudly.

"Oh no," he said.

chapter 33

Sarah sat alone in her room on Planet Royale. She felt completely and totally miserable, and she was on one of her least favorite planets. There was absolutely nothing to do besides relax, which just happened to be the thing Sarah liked doing least in the entire universe.

She had accidentally offended just about everyone in the Astral world. Mick had dumped her from the campaign. She had nowhere to turn. She thought about going home, back to her family, back to her sister The Brat and piano lessons and ballet practice and soccer matches, but there was something that was stopping her from getting on a spaceship and heading home.

Sarah Daisy was not a person who just gave up.

Sure, her career as a future vice president was over, but there were still crazy Astrals out there who wanted to destroy Earth, and she wasn't about to let them destroy her planet without putting up a fight. Jacob Wonderbar was now Earth's only hope. Sarah felt sad when she thought about him winning and never coming back home to Earth and being president, but if that was the tradeoff for having a planet to go home to, she knew what she had to do. She had to help Jacob Wonderbar win.

Sarah tried calling him on her Telly, but he wasn't picking up. She tried Dexter, and he didn't pick up either.

She wasn't about to call Princess Pointyhead. She stared at her phone and tried to figure out what to do.

Praiseworthy.

She called Praiseworthy, who picked up with a yelp, and Sarah suddenly found herself in the cockpit. She saw Jacob at the wheel of the spaceship, and Princess Catalina, Dexter, and a monkey were holding on tightly. Sarah was alarmed that Jacob was driving the ship, and she scrambled over to the cockpit window to see if he was about to crash into something. She was quite surprised to see that he was actually driving rather well.

"Daisy Mistress!" Praiseworthy yelled. "Trouble in are we!"

Sarah looked at the ceiling. "What?"

"Backward talking I'm. It help can't I."

"You're talking backward?"

"Understand you'd knew I. Intelligent so you're! Friends we're glad so I'm, Daisy Mistress, oh!"

"Praiseworthy, don't talk to Sarah!" Jacob shouted, but he was soon distracted as a bright bolt almost grazed the ship out in space. Someone was shooting at them.

"How far until Planet Blueprint?!" Dexter yelped.

"Not far!" Princess Catalina said.

Sarah didn't even have to ask Praiseworthy who was chasing them. It was definitely the Valkyrians, and Sarah was sure that Mick Cracken was behind it. Now that Mick was tanking in the polls thanks to her gaffe, the only way he had to still win the election was to kidnap Jacob Wonderbar and put him out of commission.

"Praiseworthy, what's Planet Blueprint?"

"Live workers construction where planet the it's. Royale Planet from away hours Earth four only it's. Us help please, Daisy Mistress!"

Sarah closed her eyes and concentrated in order to

decipher what Praiseworthy was saying. It's where the construction workers lived. They needed her help. It was only four Earth hours away.

"I'm on it!" she shouted. "End call."

Sarah found herself back in her room on Planet Royale. She ran down the hall toward the spaceport where the spaceship Lucy was parked, and she smiled for the first time since she had said the word "alien."

Her political career may have been down the tubes, but at least she could try to save Jacob Wonderbar. Even if he didn't want her to.

chapter 34

Jacob Wonderbar wasn't pleased that crazed Valkyrians had forced them to land on a planet of construction workers. But at least they had the monkeys.

When Boris sensed that Jacob, Catalina, and Dexter were in trouble, he planted himself by Jacob's side and never let him stray too far. He screeched orders to the other monkeys, and they began scrambling around and jumping up and down and throwing things around the hold.

Between Jacob's expert piloting and Praiseworthy's rocket boosters, they had managed to put some distance between themselves and the Valkyrians, but they wouldn't have much time before the commandos arrived.

Jacob nodded to Catalina and Dexter. Dexter punched the button that opened the door, and they stepped out onto Planet Blueprint. They had landed in a field adjacent to a large city, where nearly every building was covered in varying types of scaffolding, from metal frames covered in blue mesh to bamboo improbably stretching high into the air. There were cranes everywhere, and Jacob had never heard the sound of so many jackhammers in his life. The nearest buildings under construction had wooden fences protecting the site around ground level, and burly men and women were peeking through the holes, trying to get a glimpse at the building taking shape behind the walls.

There was a man standing near Praiseworthy wearing blue jeans and a flannel shirt. He had a thick mustache and a bit of a belly, and he was carrying a large thermos. Dozens of tools dangled from a large leather belt around his waist.

"Sir," Jacob said. "Can you help us? We're being chased! We need help."

The man reached out and rapped on the side of Praiseworthy's hull with his knuckles, then grunted in approval. Boris thumped the ground threateningly, but the construction worker didn't seem to notice.

"What you got here, a TCX-45?" the man asked.

"Um," Jacob said. "I don't really know."

The man looked at Jacob like he was rather dumb. "You mean to tell me you don't know the make and model of the ship you're driving?" the man asked.

Jacob blushed in embarrassment. It probably was something he should know. But there wasn't time to stop and chat about it.

"Wait a second, aren't you that Earther that's running for president?" the man asked.

"Yes, but—"

The man sniffed. "I'm not voting for someone who doesn't know what kind of spaceship he's driving."

There was a sudden roar in the sky, and Jacob saw the three Valkyrian ships entering the atmosphere. They had to hurry.

"Go! Go!" he shouted.

Jacob, Dexter, Catalina, and the monkeys started running through the field, but one of the Valkyrian ships quickly swooped down and landed in front of them. Its gleaming golden hull and eagle-like shape were quite intimidating.

Jacob spun around in frustration and saw the other two ships land on the other side of the field. They were surrounded, and he knew they were sitting ducks

standing in the field. They had arrived on Planet Blueprint too late, and now they were trapped. Boris stepped forward and beat his chest in the direction of the Valkyrian ship.

Jacob motioned to the others to run back to Praiseworthy. At least they could try to blast off again.

"Hey!" the construction worker standing near Praiseworthy said when the children approached. "Are those Valkyrians?"

"Yes!" Jacob shouted.

"We don't like Valkyrians here," the construction worker said.

"Why?" Dexter asked.

"Dexter, we don't have time to talk," Jacob said.

"Those Valkyrians are always blowing things up," the construction worker said. "We like to build stuff."

"Maybe you can help us!" Dexter said.

"We don't have time," Jacob said. "We need to get out of here!"

"Hang on there, kid!" The man signaled to Jacob for time. He reached around to the back of his tool belt and then showed the children a roll of duct tape, which he held carefully, as if it were a priceless, holy object. "We've got this," the man whispered.

He ran off in the direction of the nearest construction site.

Jacob shook his head. He didn't know how a construction worker was going to stop blaster-toting soldiers, no matter how many magical qualities duct tape possessed.

"Maybe we should surrender," Catalina said quietly.

Jacob immediately shook his head. "No way."

"They have us surrounded! What are we supposed to do?"

"Attention space monkeys!" a booming voice said from one of the Valkyrian ships. "We have one million bananas waiting for you on board. Come and get them!"

One of the small monkeys immediately began scrambling toward the Valkyrians. Boris rushed after him angrily and then smacked him over the head. The smaller monkey sheepishly followed Boris back toward Praiseworthy.

Jacob tried to think of how they could get away. They didn't have any weapons, and they wouldn't be able to blast off without the Valkyrians shooting them out of the sky.

"Correction, space monkeys!" the booming voice

said. "We have one *billion* bananas waiting for you! Banana now! Banana now!"

Boris jumped up and down and began running toward the Valkyrian ship. The other monkeys followed him.

"Boris, no!" Jacob shouted. He couldn't bear to think of the smug look on Patrick Gravy's face now that the space monkeys had deserted him.

When the monkeys reached the Valkyrians, instead of heading for the hold, they scrambled onto the ship. Then they began hitting it as hard as they could, denting the hull and splintering the glass on the cockpit.

"Ha-ha!" Dexter shouted. "Get 'em!"

Rufus swung from one of the ship's blasters and bent it into an odd angle.

But Jacob heard a commotion coming from one of the other ships, and a dozen commandos ran out, doing somersaults and shouting "Cover me!" and pointing their blasters all around.

"Boris!" Catalina shouted. "Look out!"

Boris screeched loudly, and the monkeys scrambled inside the Valkyrian ship. After a little while, unarmed Valkyrian soldiers were careening out of the hold, and the monkeys had clearly taken control. The nose of the ship lifted up, and even though it was damaged, it flew straight at the charging soldiers, who retreated back into their ship.

That was when Jacob felt a blaster poke into his back.

"Call the monkeys off," he heard Patrick Gravy say.

Jacob couldn't believe it. In all the noise and excitement he hadn't even heard Patrick Gravy and Madrigal sneaking up on him.

"Never," Jacob said.

Catalina grabbed Jacob's hand. "Don't be crazy! Do it, Dexter."

"Boris! Rufus!" Dexter shouted, waving his arms at the ship.

After a short while, the monkeys emerged from the ship they had commandeered and slunk toward Praiseworthy. They were quickly surrounded by Valkyrian soldiers.

"We're going to make this nice and easy," Patrick said. "You're going to disappear until this election is over, and then we'll send you on your way back to Earth. That is, if Earth still exists!"

"Ha-ha!" Madrigal laughed. "It probably won't."

"Me dear oh," Praiseworthy said.

Jacob heard a shriek. One of the soldiers was trying to put a leash on Rufus.

215

"Don't do that!" Dexter shouted.

"Let's go," Patrick said.

There was a sharp *thweep* and thud, and Jacob looked over and saw Patrick's blaster affixed to Praiseworthy with a large nail.

There was another *thweep*, and Madrigal's blaster went flying out his hand.

Jacob scanned the field and saw construction workers wielding nail guns at the edge of the clearing. They were wearing hard hats and were hiding behind a barricade made of stacked lunch pails.

"Men, get them!" Patrick shouted.

But now that Jacob, Dexter, and Catalina were out of danger, the monkeys started fighting back. Boris tackled one of the soldiers, grabbed one of the blasters, and fired it into the air randomly.

"Retreat! Retreat!" the soldiers shouted, and they ran for their ships. One of the spaceships tried to take off, but it was attached to the ground with a long, indestructible length of duct tape.

"No!" Patrick shouted. He started running after his men, with Madrigal right behind him. "Be brave, be brave!"

In a blur of monkey power, Rufus ran and tackled Patrick and pinned him to the ground. He bared his teeth and looked like he was going to bite.

Jacob and Dexter exchanged glances and then ran over. Rufus stared Patrick right in the eye.

"Please!" Patrick cried. "I'm sorry! Let me go!"

Jacob stared at Patrick for a while. He wanted nothing more than to let Rufus get revenge on Patrick, but he knew it wasn't the right thing to do. "This ends here," Jacob said. "Hear me? No more kidnapping."

"Yes!" Patrick shouted. "Anything!"

"Do you promise?"

"Yes, I promise!"

Jacob knew they shouldn't take revenge on Patrick, and he wasn't about to stoop to kidnapping him. He nodded to Dexter. He would show Patrick what Earthers were really made of.

"Let him go, Rufus," Dexter said.

"Wait," Jacob said. He leaned over and ripped one of the shiny medals off of Patrick's uniform. "Okay, now he can go."

After a moment, Rufus stood up reluctantly and let Patrick scurry away. He ran clumsily toward the nearest ship, and Jacob wondered if he'd regret showing him mercy.

He gave the medal to Dexter. "I hereby present you this medal, Colonel Goldstein, for bravery in battle."

Dexter laughed and bowed. "Accepted with honor, your lordship."

The construction worker who had been standing near Praiseworthy sauntered over to where Jacob and Dexter were standing. "Hey kids," he said. "That was a pretty manly thing to do, letting him go like that. You guys are manly men."

Dexter shook his head with a sigh. "No, we're just people."

The man nodded. "Well, you have my vote."

Jacob, Dexter, and Catalina were sitting in a field eating lunch a few hours later when they saw the spaceship Lucy high up in the sky. After the last of the Valkyrians had blasted off and left them alone, the construction workers got to work repairing Praiseworthy and gave the children metal lunch pails full of sandwiches, potato chips, and milk in a thermos.

Jacob remembered the first time he had seen the spaceship Lucy, sitting in the forest near his house, and he smiled when he thought of how happy he had been to see her when he was stuck on Numonia. He really had come a long way and had so many adventures.

Lucy touched down nearby, and Sarah Daisy

stepped out from the hold. She had her hands stuck nervously in her pockets, and she averted her eyes as she walked over.

There was an uncomfortable silence when she stood in front of them, and Jacob thought back to the time they had spoken over the Astral Telly, when she had refused to quit Mick Cracken's campaign. Now that she had been forced to resign, a significant part of him was relieved she was finally away from Mick Cracken and that things had clearly taken a turn for the worse between them.

"So what are we going to do now, Jake?" Sarah said. "How are you doing?"

"I don't know . . ." Jacob said.

The silence stretched on for a little while longer, as no one quite knew what to say. Jacob picked at a blade of grass and broke it into small pieces, staring at it intently.

Sarah tapped Catalina on the shoulder. "Hey. Sorry I called you an al . . ." Sarah said. "Well, you know."

Catalina gave her a fake smile. "That's all right, sweetie, I know you can't help your terrible manners."

Sarah fumed, but Jacob knew that if she could apologize to her worst enemy, they could all be friends again. He stood up and gave Sarah a hug. "It's really good to see you," he said, and he meant it.

Sarah nodded, and said, "You too." She broke off the hug and gave Dexter a shove. "C'mere weirdo," she said, and they hugged as well.

She sat down with them and ate some of Jacob's potato chips. Catalina watched her every move.

"So . . . Seriously, what are you going to do now?" Sarah asked.

"Well," Jacob said. "I need to get ready for the third Battle Supreme. And I was thinking maybe we could get a few last appearances in before the election. We don't have much time."

Sarah stopped chewing, and looked at Jacob with a panicked expression. She swallowed with difficulty and said very quietly, "Oh no, oh no . . . I asked you 'What are you going to do,' but you thought . . . Oh Jake, you haven't heard."

"Heard what?"

Sarah's mouth quivered. "I'm really sorry, Jake. I saw it on my Telly right before I got here and I thought you knew. I'm so sorry, I know how badly you wanted to be president. This is all my fault."

Jacob's face felt fuzzy. He didn't like the way she was talking about his campaign in the past tense. "What do you mean 'wanted to be president'?"

Sarah stared at the ground. "Well, you know after I

called Catalina an A-word, and after that stupid traitor dumped me from the campaign, Mick went and gave a speech talking about the 'Earth Menace' and how dangerous Earth is to Astrals. I know he doesn't mean it and is just trying to get Astrals all riled up, but it worked. People got really upset, talking about how Earth is going to go to war with Astrals.

"And then . . ." She wiped her eyes and cleared her voice. "Then he announced a new rule, which he had pushed through the Election Council."

Jacob's heart was racing. "What rule?" he asked.

Sarah sighed. "Earthers aren't allowed to run for president. No one is going to be allowed to vote for you. He stole the election."

Jacob leaned back slowly and lay down on the ground, staring at the sky. It wasn't happening. It couldn't possibly be happening. He felt sick, exhausted, and drained. Everything he had worked for. All those campaign events and speeches and interviews. All for nothing. Mick had done it in just a few hours. He had outsmarted him, and all of Jacob's efforts were in vain.

He had come so far. After Sarah's gaffe he really thought he was going to win. He had pulled pranks and eaten corndogs and was about to win fair and square. He had made Astrals get to know him, and even made them think he was one of them.

Of course Mick would stack the deck against him. Mick couldn't win on his own, so he had to cheat.

He felt Sarah's hand on his shoulder. "I'm sorry, Jake."

chapter 36

What are we going to do?" Dexter asked.

They were sitting aboard Praiseworthy flying aimlessly through space while they tried to figure out where to go and what they could possibly do about the situation. Catalina didn't think it was likely that they would be able to sway the Election Council, and an appeal to the king would be futile because he had already handed control over to the council. Jacob figured there was only one possibility remaining.

"Catalina should take my place," Jacob said. "I'll be a special adviser or something. She's an Astral, she can be president."

Catalina smiled. "That's really sweet, Jacob, but I don't want to be president. That would be so boring. I want to be a princess."

Jacob gritted his teeth. "Catalina, you are really smart. You could be president. Don't you want to be something? You'd rather just let your brother win than try and be your own person?"

Catalina shook her head. "Jacob, darling, I'm not one of those people who doesn't realize how good she has it. Being a princess is *wonderful*."

"But how are you going to be princess if Mick is president? He's getting rid of the whole monarchy. Isn't it time to give up the princess thing?"

Catalina shook her head again and tried to look confident, but Jacob sensed she was questioning herself. "Oh, well. I . . . I know how to take care of my brother. Don't you worry about a thing."

Jacob rolled his eyes. It didn't make any sense. It seemed like she was in total denial that her old life of tea parties and crowns was coming to an end.

"At least I got to spend time with you, darling!" she said. "How are we going to get married someday if we don't get to know each other?"

Jacob looked over at Sarah Daisy, whose face was bright red and who looked capable of extreme violence.

"So I guess this is it then," Jacob said.

Jacob's Telly buzzed to life. He looked at it, and

when he saw who it was, he felt like he was going to faint.

"It's the king."

"The king? Really?!" Dexter said.

"The king is calling you?!" Sarah asked.

"He's sending me an invite to talk at the palace."

"Answer it, silly!" Catalina said. "And tell Daddy I say hello!"

Jacob took a deep breath and said, "Accept" and felt his mind whisked away to Planet Royale. He found himself in the garden with the king, who was staring at a fountain and was dressed in bright red robes. There was a light rain falling and the king didn't seem to mind, but Jacob found it very strange to be standing in the rain without feeling the raindrops or getting wet at all.

"Hello, Jacob," the king said.

"Hi," Jacob managed to say, looking around the garden.

The king stared at Jacob for a while and then said, "Have you ever wondered why Astrals like you so much?"

Jacob furrowed his brow. "Um . . . No?"

"You came into the election at an enormous disadvantage, given the skepticism Astrals have about

people from Earth. And yet you made an impressive comeback, particularly given your . . . slow start. Why do you think that was?"

Jacob had been so consumed by the campaign that he hadn't even really thought about it that much. "Well," he said. "I guess I realized at some point that I needed to be myself and trust my instincts. And that even if I was going to lose I should at least just get that one thing right. That started working."

The king looked impressed. "Quite right," he said. "Quite right. Though sometimes even one's best isn't enough, is it?"

Jacob didn't know how to answer that, and the king turned and walked away. Jacob followed, and they arrived at a statue of a spaceship. The king stared at it for a moment before turning back to Jacob. "I suppose you've heard about the rule that bars Earthers from running for office. What do you plan to do about it?"

Jacob hadn't thought there was anything he *could* do about it, but since the king asked, he started thinking. "I guess I can try to get it overturned. Or maybe steal your time machine and go back and stop Sarah from saying the A-word."

The king smiled. "That's what I thought you'd say.

But Jacob, I don't think the situation calls for that type of a solution."

Jacob waited for the king to tell him he could just go back to his life on Earth. To let him down easy, tell him that it was a good run and that he was proud of him. A part of him would have found it a terrific relief for the king to just say that Jacob had done well, but there was nothing he could do and everything was over. Even the king didn't have power in the new era, so it was time to go home. But another part was mad that Mick was taking away the Astrals' first chance to choose their leader instead of inheriting one. It was going to be Mick Cracken or nothing. Mick had seen to that.

"Jacob, the new rule says that no Earther can be president."

Jacob nodded.

"But you're not an Earther. Well, not entirely."

Jacob felt his entire body go numb. Of course he was an Earther! He grew up on Earth and his parents were . . . He stopped his train of thought and thought about his father and the strange postcard and the pipe he had found on Planet Paisley and how Jacob had always suspected that his father might actually be lost in outer space. If Jacob wasn't "entirely" an Earther, that meant . . .

"Jacob, you are half Astral. And you are still very eligible for this election."

chapter 37

Just two Earth days later, Jacob found himself competing in the third Battle Supreme. The final battle was administered at the sole discretion of the king, who had given away no hints of what he had in store for Jacob and Mick.

Jacob had barely gotten used to the fact that he was still in the race, and he was incredibly furious at Mick, who had reached new depths of dirty deeds and bad sportsmanship, even by Mick's extremely low moral standards.

But Jacob knew he had to focus on winning the last battle. It was anybody's election to win, particularly since Astrals had taken very kindly to the announcement that Jacob was partly one of them. Mick was clinging to the narrowest of leads in the polls.

The king stood up from his throne and the room hushed. Jacob detected just a hint of melancholy in the king's demeanor, but he still held himself with his usual confident and regal bearing.

"Welcome, everyone, to the third Battle Supreme. Before we begin, I'd like to take this opportunity to thank you for bestowing on me the honor of leading such a wonderful community of space humans for all these years. I have no reservations whatsoever about leaving Astrals in the care of one of these two fine young men. There can, of course, be only one winner, but I have every confidence that whichever of them you choose to lead you will do so with honor and dignity. Thank you, thank you, everyone."

Jacob immediately stood up and clapped, and others in the room followed suit. After a moment, Mick grudgingly stood up and clapped as well.

"Thank you," the king said, and Jacob noted a new glint in his eye. "Now, you are all probably wondering what we have in store for the last Battle Supreme. Well, it is quite simple. I want Jacob and Mick to show us which of them wants to be president the most."

There was a murmur in the crowd. Jacob glared at Mick, who met his eyes and smirked.

"They say that where a man's treasure lies, there you'll find his heart. Michaelus Crackenarium, the

physical object you value the most is your spaceship, Mick Jr."

The smile on Mick's face waned. Jacob knew he hated to hear the sound of his real name.

"Jacob Wonderbar, the physical object you value the most is your grandfather's pipe."

The king snapped his fingers, and images of both objects were projected onto two large screens. "These are live recordings. I have rigged the spaceship Mick Jr. and the Wonderbar pipe with explosives."

The king handed small handheld devices to both Jacob and Mick. "And these are the triggers to the explosives. The first candidate to blow up their prized possession will show us that they want to win this election more than their opponent. The third Battle Supreme starts now."

At that, the king sat down.

"What?" Jacob gulped.

"Whoa," he heard Dexter say in the audience.

It couldn't be true. The king really wanted him to destroy his dad's pipe? Jacob had so many memories about that pipe, and now that he knew his dad really was an Astral, it meant more to him than ever. It had belonged to his grandfather, an imposing man Jacob's dad had said was German, but Jacob realized in his flash that the reason his grandfather had had a faint accent must have been because he was an Astral. The pipe was Jacob's connection to space and to his Astral heritage, and no matter how much he wanted to win the election, and no matter how frustrated and disappointed he was by his father, that pipe was bound up with so many emotions and memories and mysteries. His mom didn't take many pictures when he was growing up, and there wasn't any trace of his father left. He couldn't bear to press the trigger on the one thing he had left that belonged to his dad. It might as well have been a choice to blow up his own father.

He glanced over at Mick Cracken, who was clearly doing some soul-searching of his own. A bead of sweat dripped down his forehead. Jacob knew Mick loved that ship more than anything, and after Jacob had defaced it, Mick had used the time in the shop to not only restore it to perfection, but to add still more enhancements.

Neither of them wanted to destroy the object they prized the most, but Jacob had a feeling that Mick would go first.

And when he thought about it, Jacob had to admit that Mick probably did want to win the election more than he did. Mick wanted it more than anything in the entire universe. He had been the one to convince the king to have elections, and he had been thinking about and preparing for the election for his entire life. The more Jacob thought about it, he realized there was no doubt about which one of them wanted it more. It was definitely Mick.

But then an image of Earth popped into his head. Could he really be so selfish that he wouldn't blow up a pipe when it meant saving his planet?

Jacob didn't know what to do, but he knew he had to trust his heart. He could lose the battle and still win the election. He had to be himself.

Mick held up the trigger, and Jacob heard him whisper, "Three . . . two . . ."

"Stop!" Jacob shouted. He threw his trigger away so there was no doubt about his intentions. "Don't do it."

The room silenced, and Mick paused.

"There's no need to blow up your spaceship. You want this more than I do. I'm forfeiting this battle. You win this one. But *just* this one."

Mick raised his fist in triumph and basked in the applause, and the sight of Mick Cracken's patented smirk almost made Jacob run over and blow up Mick Jr. himself. After a few moments of gloating, Mick suddenly realized something and said, "If anyone tells Mick Jr. about this, I will have you arrested when I'm president."

"I'm still going to win," Jacob snapped.

The king stepped up to the platform and signaled for attention. "Splendid show, candidates, splendid show. However, I must remind Candidate Wonderbar that it isn't within his rights to forfeit this battle, as I am the sole and final judge. And I haven't yet had my say."

Jacob wasn't sure where the king was going with his speech, and from the murmuring throughout the room, he could tell he wasn't alone.

"In my experience, the best leaders are not the ones who desire power the most, who crave attention, or who most want to be in charge. Leading isn't about winning, it is about doing what is right. The best leaders are humble, selfless, and wise. They might not even really want to be leaders in the first place. This Battle Supreme was a test of the challengers' humility. I intended all along to reward the candidate who wanted to win the least, because the less you *want* to be a leader, the better leader you shall be."

The king paused.

"And therefore I declare Jacob Wonderbar the winner of the third Battle Supreme."

Sarah, Dexter, and Catalina screamed their applause. The rest of the room started speaking at once in confusion.

236

Mick slammed the trigger to the ground, and yelled, "I hate you!" at his father. The room quieted. Once again, Jacob had seen the king step on the dreams of his own son, and even though he was grateful for the victory, Jacob was beginning to wonder if the king was as fair and good as he had once thought. It seemed like a trick designed solely to humiliate Mick Cracken.

Even though he had just won the third Battle Supreme and the presidency was tantalizingly close, Jacob couldn't help but feel a little bit bad for Mick.

chapter 38

As Jacob finished up his speech laying out his vision for a new Astral nation that was at peace with Earth, it felt surreal knowing that he was at his last campaign event. It was the night before the election, and he had come so far. He'd been gone for two Earth weeks, and the next day he would either be voted president of the universe or . . . nothing.

Leader in charge of everything that exists, the first president in Astral history . . . or just another seventh grader at Magellan Middle School.

He tried picturing the future, and it was like there were two screens, one where the Astrals voted him president and he lived on Planet Royale and passed laws and was the most important and powerful person alive. And then on the other screen was homework and school and substitute teachers and chores and other drudgery, but also more time with his mom and Sarah Daisy and Dexter Goldstein, and shooting hoops until it got dark and laughing at the movies and summer vacations doing whatever he wanted.

Jacob stared out at the crowd that had gathered on Planet Royale to hear him speak, and he just felt so tired. He found Sarah in the crowd, and when they locked eyes he remembered their conversation before they blasted off.

"What if you win?" she had asked.

What if you win?

What if you are in charge of every planet and every person everywhere? What if you can't sleep at night because you're thinking about the hungry people out there and the sad people and the hurt people and the ones who want to blow up planets because they're crazy and they're all your responsibility? What if you never have time for fun and your friends and relaxing and everyone is constantly criticizing you because they think they could do your job better?

What if you win?

Jacob did his final waves to the crowd and ducked backstage. He stood in a corner and put his face in his hands and tried to make sense of what he was feeling. The room was a tangled mess of activity, but Jacob

just wanted to disappear. Boris was scurrying around pushing people and checking badges to make sure everyone was authorized to be in the room, Dexter was teaching Rufus how to do a cartwheel, and Catalina swooped over to give Jacob a hug.

"Darling, that was amazing! I think it was your best speech yet! I agree that Astrals shouldn't be scared of Earth! I did some research, and you even have some passable fashion designers."

"Thanks," Jacob mumbled.

Over Catalina's shoulder, Jacob saw Sarah Daisy enter the room and stop, her face slowly turning red as she saw Jacob hugging Catalina.

Jacob broke the hug and cleared his voice. "Hey, everyone?" he said. The room immediately silenced, which Jacob found incredibly strange. Who was he to make everyone quiet at the merest sound of his voice? He was just a seventh grader from Magellan Middle School who liked corndogs and happened to have a father from outer space.

"Hey, everyone, I just wanted to thank you for everything you've done for this campaign. I just really, really appreciate it. You didn't have to do it, and you did it, and that means so much to me."

And as he looked out at everyone, he realized how far everyone had come for him and how much they

had given up. How much time and energy Catalina had put into the campaign, how Dexter had found his own way back and taken care of the monkeys as best he could, and how even Sarah Daisy returned to help him out for the final days of the campaign.

They did it all for him. And if he somehow came up short when the votes came in, all of their work would be for nothing. He would fail them and everyone on Earth. He wasn't sure how he would be able to face it.

"Hey, so . . ." Jacob said. "Could I speak to Sarah alone?"

Catalina whipped her head around and stared at Sarah for a moment, before she laughed and said, "Of course, darling. Whatever you need."

Dexter led the monkeys out, Catalina followed the monkeys, and some of the Planet Royale servants who had been making sure Jacob had everything he needed quietly slipped away as well.

Jacob was alone with Sarah, and he tried to get the courage to say what he needed to say.

"Jake," Sarah said. "Whatever you want to say . . . If this is about your dad—"

"I don't know if I want to win," Jacob blurted out.

He couldn't look her in the eye. The entire Planet Earth needed him to win. There were crazy SEERs out there who wanted nothing more than to blow up

his planet, and Mick Cracken cared too much about being president to stop them. His friends were counting on him, and the fate of the entire planet was resting on his shoulders. And instead he was thinking about playing sports and hanging out with his friends and . . . being a kid.

"I got so wrapped up in it," Jacob said quickly. "I mean, the king wanted me to run. The king. How could I say no to that? And Earth . . . I know I have to win, but I just can't shake the feeling that I don't know if I want to. It's just too much. Maybe Dexter was right. Maybe I'm not presidential material."

Sarah reached out and grabbed his hand. And unlike their conversation over the Telly a week ago, this time their hands really touched. He felt the warmth of her palm and knew she was really, truly there.

"Jake, whatever happens, we'll support you. We'll still be your friends. Me and Dexter. You know that, right? Even . . . Miss Twinkle Toes," she said with great effort. "We're here for you. And you know, the king sort of said you're not even supposed to *want* to win."

Jacob was so glad she was back with him. And as he saw how fragile Sarah looked, her eyes worried and her lips pressed, it occurred to him how hard the last few days had to have been for her too, with the entire

universe suddenly deciding they didn't like her just because she said something she didn't even mean. And yet even with all that going on, Sarah was still trying to make *him* feel better.

"Sarah, I'm sorry about everything. That whole 'A' thing was so stupid. You didn't deserve that."

Sarah shrugged. "Yeah. It was stupid. But sometimes bad things happen, Jake, and you can spend your time worrying about them or you can just try and make sure the next day is better than the last one."

Jacob nodded. Whatever happened in the election, he knew he could handle it. Whether he was in charge of the universe or just another kid living on a boring street, deep down he knew he would still be the same person, only better off for having tried for this one big thing.

He wished they could go home, so he could be with his mom while everyone voted and so he could sleep in his own bed, but he knew it wouldn't be practical to get all the way back through the space kapow detour, and who knows what the Valkyrians still had planned for him. He had to spend at least one more day in outer space, and then if he won, he had to get ready for the entire universe to be his responsibility. He couldn't go home to Earth.

But he suddenly thought of the next best thing.

chapter 39

On the day of the vote that would decide the fate of the first presidential election in Astral history, Jacob Wonderbar felt squishy dirt under his feet, couldn't see anything exciting on the horizon, and had never felt so glad to smell burp breath in his entire life.

He wasn't home, but at least he was on Numonia.

The monkeys weren't sure how they felt about the lack of gravity, but soon took to engaging in ever-more-spectacular wrestling matches. Dexter picked up a clump of Numonia space dust and hurled it at Rufus, which introduced an entirely new weapon into space monkey warfare. Princess Catalina stepped daintily around and tried to lock a smile on her face and be a good sport.

Jacob just wanted to introduce Sarah Daisy to Moonman and Stargirl.

"They're just . . ." Jacob said. "Well . . . I probably can't do them justice, I'd—"

They heard a whoop, and for a brief moment Jacob saw Moonman and Stargirl illuminated against the ever-so-brief Numonian sunset, their large bodies conveying pure joy. Then night came and they were plunged into darkness.

"It's them!"

He ran in their direction, and caught up to them just as they were awakening from their thirty-second slumber.

Stargirl grabbed Jacob into a powerful and long hug, and he felt so happy to be with them. She held him by the shoulders and Jacob saw tears of happiness in her eyes.

"I told Moonman you'd come back," Stargirl wept. "I knew you would, Jacob. I just knew it."

"I'm so glad to be here," Jacob said, and he really meant it. They were so nice and they cared about him so much, and all he wanted to do was show Sarah how amazing they were.

"Now hold on there," Moonman said, noticing Sarah. "We haven't met this lovely young lady."

Jacob said with pride, "Moonman, Stargirl, I'd like you to meet—"

Just then the sun set behind the horizon, Numonia was plunged into darkness, and Moonman and Stargirl fell fast asleep.

Jacob laughed and said, "Yeah, this happens."

"They seem so nice," Sarah said.

Jacob nodded. "They really are."

Jacob smiled at Sarah in the Numonian darkness, but he wasn't sure if she saw it. They waited patiently until Moonman and Stargirl awoke, then Jacob was finally able to introduce Sarah.

"Any friend of Jacob Wonderbar's is a friend of ours," Moonman said proudly. "And I suspect you're going to like it here."

After they had eaten a Numonian feast, during which even Jacob was able to slowly choke down some morsels of Numonian space dust, they all filed over to the spaceship Swift, where the Numonians had created a makeshift voting booth hidden away by a mound of Numonian dust.

"Not that we need any privacy," Moonman said, puffing out his chest and slapping Jacob on the back. "We all know who is going to win on this planet."

When Jacob faced the presidential voting buttons, he stared at his name, knowing that on that very day many billions of Astrals were all looking at his name on a button too. All the campaigning, all the speeches, all the

interviews, it all came down to a bunch of people pushing a button with either his or Mick Cracken's name.

Jacob braced himself and said, "Conference" to his Telly and suddenly he was surrounded by reporters shouting his name and taking pictures. One last photo shoot as Candidate Wonderbar.

Jacob pushed the voting button. It registered, and he had cast one more vote for saving Earth.

He gave a confident thumbs-up to the reporters, made sure they got some good footage, and then said, "End conference." He was alone again.

Jacob tuned in on his Telly and watched the coverage as people voted all around the galaxy. There were polling stations in trees, in bus stops, on construction sites, and atop skyscrapers. Everyone was voting, even kids Jacob's age, and they did it with a sense of purpose, seeming to know that even if any one person probably wasn't casting the vote that was going to decide everything, they were doing something important together. They were choosing their leader, rather than just following whoever was next in the Crackenarium family tree.

And even as Moonman and Stargirl and old man Bartholomew and the other Numonians fell asleep every thirty seconds during the coverage, they all huddled in front of a screen on the spaceship Swift and watched the final results.

On Planet Royale, amid a great fanfare of trumpets blaring, colorful birds flying, and a giant new tapestry swinging down from the ceiling to commemorate the election, they saw the king of everything step up to a dais and begin to speak. Moonman told everyone to hush, then fell asleep and started snoring.

"For the first time in their history, Astrals have chosen their own leader," the king said. "The first Astral leader was Father Albert, my many-many-times-great-

grandfather, who led our people into the stars. And now, for the first time in our storied history, Astrals will decide for themselves who will lead them to a safe and prosperous future."

Jacob's heart was pounding. It was time for the results. He only had one thought. President of the universe or nothing. President of the universe or nothing.

"The votes have been counted. The will of the Astrals has been written."

Jacob closed his eyes. President of the universe or nothing. President of the universe or nothing.

"You have chosen your leader."

President of the universe or nothing. President of the universe or nothing.

"And it gives me a great deal of pleasure to announce . . . that *Mick Cracken* will be the first president of the universe!"

Jacob let the news wash over him. He had to replay the moment in his mind several times to be sure he had heard correctly, and every time he played it back in his head, he heard the king say Mick's name.

President of the universe or nothing. President of the universe or nothing.

Jacob wasn't president.

But he didn't feel like nothing.

chapter 40

The planet of Numonia was completely silent once Moonman shut off the old-fashioned video screen. Jacob was so worried about Earth and what losing meant for his home planet that it took him a little while to notice everyone darting their eyes at him to see how he was reacting. Not actually staring, but finding things on the other side of the wall that attracted their attention and ever so briefly flickering their eyes over him to see how he was taking the loss.

He didn't want or need their sympathy. It somehow made it worse to think that everyone felt sorry for him. Their pity itself was a constant reminder that he hadn't succeeded and that they knew exactly how bad he felt. Even if the attention was very kind, he wanted things to just go back to normal. He was far less devastated than he thought he would have been.

Yes, it was bad, it was embarrassing and difficult to lose, but he would get through it.

He was still Jacob Wonderbar.

Jacob stood up quickly. "Everyone, I'm fine. I really am. I mean it."

He looked around the room and could feel everyone's disbelief.

"Guys!" he shouted, and everyone snapped to life. "It's okay, I'm just—"

But he couldn't finish the sentence.

He knew he would be fine. He had run an incredible campaign, one that he would be proud of forever.

Except for one thing, one crucial thing, which he felt slipping away yet again.

Jacob turned away from his friends and walked out of the spaceship Swift and into the Numonian night. He stared at the electric glow of his Telly.

He knew he'd probably never again be as famous as he was at that moment. His name had been on every news program and part of nearly every topic of conversation, everywhere in the galaxy. Everyone had known who he was, where he was, and what he was doing throughout the entire election.

And still his dad had never called. Jacob thought for sure that at some point his dad would finally reach out to him, to tell him he was proud of his campaign or at least to explain why he never showed up after he sent the postcard.

Jacob was so tired of waiting for a moment that might never come. He would have to call his dad.

He summoned his courage. It was just a phone call. He stared at his Telly, then said, "Call Dad."

He waited for his mind to be transported to wherever his dad was in outer space, someplace where his dad was lost or amid some situation that was somehow preventing him from being a dad. Jacob braced himself for the anger he would feel when his dad picked up, and prepared to scream, "Why do I have to be the one calling you?!"

But no one picked up. The Telly beeped its failure.

Jacob tried again, but with the same result. Then he tried one more time. When that didn't work he screamed and threw his Telly away as hard as he could and sat down in the Numonian dust.

His dad wasn't there. As usual.

He should have been angry. He should have been crying. He should have felt some deep hurt and pain. But he wasn't feeling any of those things.

He didn't need his father.

And with sudden clarity, he realized that while everyone was busy worrying so much about him and how upset he was and while he had been so focused on his dad, there was something more important he could do to set things right.

He could still save Planet Earth from getting blown to smithereens.

chapter 41

Jacob's plan was in motion when he attended Mick's inauguration with Sarah, Catalina, Dexter, and the monkeys, whom Dexter somehow persuaded to wear ties for the occasion.

The ceremony was held on a royal cruise liner, and the events surrounding the swearing in had been carefully planned by the king himself. Mick and the king stood in front of a massive window that looked out into space, the stars bright and impossibly numerous and close, almost as if they were audience members watching the ceremony themselves. Mick wore a black suit with a sparkling silver tie, and the king wore golden robes.

"The stars have given us our lives," the king said to the audience, which hushed at the sound of his soft voice. "The stars don't just watch over us, they give us the energy to grow our food and warm our planets. They allow us to live among them for our brief flicker of life. More than that, they are inside all of us. Many of the atoms that make up our bodies were born in the heart of supernovas. They are a part of us. They guide us, light our way, and give us life."

The king gestured to the backdrop of stars through the large window. "And so it is with the stars watching over us that Mick Cracken takes his oath of office as the president of the universe. For he is bound to two authorities alone: the will of the Astral people, and the stars, the givers of life."

Mick nodded solemnly, and Jacob was mildly surprised to see him taking things so seriously. Even though Jacob had been trying to focus on his plan and avoid thinking about the fact that he hadn't won, he couldn't help but picture himself in Mick's shoes, with the king swearing him in and giving him the keys to the universe. As much as he had already tried to move on, there was a part of him that still wished he had won.

"Please raise your right hand," the king said, and Mick followed his instruction. "Do you swear on the stars to serve the Astral people, to hold their needs foremost, and to abide by their will?"

Mick said, "I do."

As Mick said his first "I do," Sarah edged closer to Jacob and leaned into him a bit with her shoulder.

"Do you swear on the stars that you will protect the Astral people from harm and keep them safe from all their enemies, whether from outside our community or from within?"

Jacob recoiled at this oath, and even Mick paused for a moment after hearing it. Mick turned to face the audience and locked eyes with Jacob. His face was indecipherable, and Jacob wasn't sure if Mick was thinking of him as an enemy or a friend.

"I do," Mick said.

"And do you swear on the stars that you will work to make the universe a better place, and ensure that human beings are responsible stewards of the space that the stars have given us to live in?"

"I do," Mick said.

"In order to become president, by the rules established by the Election Council you must name a vice president. Whom do you choose?"

Mick gritted his teeth a little and muttered, "Catalina Penelope Cassandra Crakenarium."

The crowd chattered with excitement, and Jacob's jaw dropped. Mick was naming his sister vice presi-

dent? Jacob looked over at Catalina and she winked at him.

The king reached over and picked up a scepter that was resting on a small altar. It had a piercing light at the end that radiated strong bright silver beams, very much like a star. He tapped it on Mick's shoulders and then handed it to him.

"Then by the authority of the stars and the Astral people, I hereby abdicate all power, give up the throne, and declare Mick Cracken president of the universe!"

The crowd gave a strong cheer at the pronouncement, and Jacob imagined the billions of people watching throughout the universe. After a moment he joined in and clapped respectfully. Sarah reluctantly clapped too.

Jacob searched the king's face for some sign of how he was feeling now that he was no longer a king, for some hint of why he gave up the throne and what his motivation had been.

And after a moment, Jacob suddenly realized what the king was thinking: He was proud. After nominating Jacob for president, after seeming to favor him and awarding him victory in the third Battle Supreme, the king was instead really, truly, unabashedly proud that his son had won.

The king didn't really intend for Jacob to win after all. Jacob thought back to what Dexter had said about why the king had nominated Jacob for president. The king had said, "Because the survival of the Planet Earth depends on it."

But that wasn't the same thing as winning.

The king had tested Mick and sent his biggest foe to run against him to challenge him, and perhaps taught him some lessons in the process. But as the king cheered on Mick Cracken's victory and stared at him not as the king but as the father of the president of the universe, Jacob knew that the king had wanted his son Mick to win all along.

chapter 42

mick Cracken stood in front of the assembled crowd and basked in the glow of achieving his life's dream, ready to give his acceptance speech. As Jacob braced himself for what he was sure would be an insufferable bit of oration, he wasn't sure he had ever seen someone so satisfied, so happy, and so completely full of himself.

"This," Mick said, unable to contain his biggest grin. "This is mind-boggling. This is unreal. This is history in the making. This is unprecedented. This is everything I hoped it would be and more. I'm . . . so incredibly awesome."

He sighed and looked as if he might pass out from joy, but then he grew more serious and raised a finger. "But this isn't about me," he said unconvincingly.

"No. This is about you, the Astral people, and . . ."

There was a gasp and a scream at the back of the crowd. People began shouting, and the lights in the room suddenly dimmed. The crowd parted to allow Patrick and General Gravy to walk to the stage. They seemed to have acquired still more medals and ribbons and were carrying very large blasters. Jacob glanced around as Valkyrian soldiers trained their blasters on the crowd. The monkeys hissed and screeched in displeasure.

As the entire crowd nervously watched the Gravys to see what they would do, Patrick slowly reached his hand up and snapped his fingers.

The window that had been showing the canopy of stars turned opaque and images of Earth flashed to life. Jacob recognized pictures of war on Earth, of bombs exploding, men shooting assault rifles, and nuclear missiles being transported on a huge truck. He also caught footage of an Arnold Schwarzenegger action movie mixed in, and he wasn't sure if the Astrals could really tell the difference.

"The Earthers are preparing to destroy us," Patrick Gravy said. "We know their war-like tendencies. It is written in their destinies. Their history has been filled with nothing but war, which has just been practice for the battles they will soon bring to space. They think we're nothing but aliens." The crowd gasped at his use of the A-word. "And it is time we Astrals protected ourselves. The day for Earther Rapture has arrived."

The window changed to show an image of Earth covered with crosshairs.

"A promise is a promise, *President* Cracken," General Gravy said in his gravelly voice. "Our missiles are ready."

Jacob locked eyes with the king, who nodded solemnly.

Jacob started walking toward the front of the stage. He had known this moment was coming. Everything was happening according to his plan.

The Gravys trained their blasters on Jacob. Patrick Gravy shouted, "Don't you dare step up to that microphone!"

Jacob summoned all of his courage and steadied his nerves as he ignored Patrick and walked to the front of the stage. Patrick fired a shot that hit the lectern, and Jacob forced himself to face death and stand fast. He didn't think that the Gravys would really shoot him in front of the largest television audience in Astral

history, but it didn't make it any easier to stand his ground. His heart pounded.

Jacob turned and pointed at the image of Earth.

"That is my home. That is where my mom lives, where my friends' families live, and where I go to school. It's a really nice planet, full of really great people. We're not perfect, and yes, there are too many wars. But we don't want to start a war with you. We want to live in peace."

"Lies!" Patrick Gravy shouted.

Jacob snapped his fingers and an image of a puppy filled the screen, followed by a rainbow over a green hill, and then nice-looking people from Earth.

"If you destroy Planet Earth, my mom will die. My mom." Jacob tried not to cry at the thought of his mom making a sandwich in the kitchen only to be blown up by crazy Valkyrians. "Lots of moms will die, and dads and friends and grandfathers and grandmothers and . . . just people. We're just people."

He snapped his fingers again, and the screen showed a corndog.

"And we eat corndogs too."

"Don't listen to him," Patrick Gravy said. "That's what the Earthers want you to think."

"You almost elected me president," Jacob said. "And that means so much to me. Astrals, you know

me. I'm half Astral. You can trust me. Don't do this."

There was another commotion in the back of the room, and Officers Bosendorfer and Erard entered with a dozen similarly rotund space officers. They trained their blasters on the Valkyrians, who began yelling at each other to hold their fire.

Jacob turned to Mick, who was watching the scene unfold with his hands clasped. There was only so much Jacob could do. At the end of the day Mick was president, and Jacob could only hope that he would make the right decision.

"Your move, Cracken," Jacob said.

Mick stepped up to the microphone and tapped his foot. He turned back to look at Earth and then looked out at the crowd, and after a moment Jacob realized he was staring at Sarah Daisy.

Mick glanced at Jacob and then shook his head slowly. "A promise is a promise," he said.

Jacob clenched his fists. He had miscalculated. He should never have trusted Mick Cracken's better judgment. That conceited space pirate was really going to . . .

"And I promised Sarah Daisy that I wouldn't let Earth be destroyed."

Jacob unclenched his hands in relief. Mick grinned at Jacob, gloating that he had tricked him.

Patrick Gravy gasped. "You promised us that you would let us destroy that stupid planet!"

Mick shrugged. "She's prettier than you are."

Suddenly Patrick turned and trained his blaster straight at Sarah, who screamed. Jacob dove off the stage and plowed into Patrick, pushing him to the ground. Patrick's blaster scattered safely away. At that precise moment the monkeys began throwing chairs and campaign paraphernalia at the Valkyrian soldiers. Boris quickly descended on General Gravy and bit his right hand until the general dropped his blaster.

"Officers Bosendorfer and Erard!" Mick shouted. "Arrest these filthy Valkyrians."

"On what charges?!" General Gravy scoffed.

Mick paused. "Destroying a defenseless moon that wasn't bothering anyone."

"Ha!" General Gravy laughed. "How about the fact that you ordered us to kidnap Jacob Wonderbar? I'm sure the courts will look kindly on that."

"That's not true," Jacob said to the crowd, grimacing at the lie he was about to tell to help Mick Cracken. "I staged those kidnappings to try and win votes. It was a campaign stunt."

"You . . ." Patrick Gravy muttered from underneath Jacob. "You liar!"

Officer Bosendorfer grabbed General Gravy roughly

by the shoulders, and Officer Erard swung Patrick up into a standing position. Officer Bosendorfer had tears in his eyes.

"I've been waiting for this moment for so long," he wept.

Officer Erard nodded and held his hand to his chest. "I always get emotional during a good arrest."

The space officers led the Valkyrians out of the room, and the audience cheered wildly. Jacob nodded his thanks to Mick, who looked happier than ever.

"Only five minutes into my presidency and already my first scandal!" Mick said.

chapter 43

"I didn't *really* want to save Earth," Mick said as the children sat in the sun on the patio at the newly renovated presidential palace on Planet Royale. Jacob and Sarah rolled their eyes at each other and Dexter scoffed. Catalina seemed distracted by Mortimer, the pink dolphin.

"I was totally ready to blow it up," Mick said. "Still might, in fact."

"Then why didn't you?" Dexter asked.

Mick jerked his thumb at Jacob. "Mr. 'My Mommy Is on Earth' made it politically impossible. The voters would have hated me for it. But I really would have done it. That whole Sarah thing was just political cover."

Everyone rolled their eyes.

"You're so full of it, Cracken," Dexter said.

Sarah and Jacob laughed in surprise. Jacob never would have thought there would be a day when Dexter would be able to stand up to Mick Cracken. Dexter really had changed.

Jacob rested his head back on his chaise longue and thought about going home to his mom and sleeping away an entire week. He knew that wouldn't be possible because there was school and homework and chores and all sorts of other menial tasks awaiting him on Earth, but at least he wasn't facing endless meetings and trips around the universe like Mick was about to endure now that he was president. The elections for the Astral Congress were just a few starweeks away, and Jacob was a bit relieved that working with a new government wasn't his problem.

"So . . ." Jacob said. "I guess this is it."

The children glanced around at one another and then looked away, not quite sure how to say good-bye.

Princess Catalina stood up first and reached out her hand to Jacob. "Can I talk to you?"

They walked together in the gardens, and Jacob wondered what Catalina would say. He knew she was facing an uncertain future, no longer a princess and now Mick's vice president, and he wondered how she had convinced Mick to name her his number two.

Princess Catalina stopped walking, and for a moment all of her composure and confidence slipped away and a tear slid down her cheek. She looked at Jacob with pained eyes, then averted them toward the ground.

"I wish you liked me as much as I like you," she said quietly. Her words stabbed Jacob more than he thought was possible. He wished he did too. She was really great, he admired her intelligence and determination, and he felt bad that he was often so frustrated by her and didn't return her feelings in the same way.

But just as suddenly as Catalina's brash and confident exterior had vanished, it was back. She tucked her hair behind her ear and straightened Jacob's collar. She gave him a dazzling smile and said, "But darling, there's still plenty of time for that. We have a whole lifetime ahead of us."

Jacob hugged Catalina and said, "Thank you so much. You're . . . amazing. You really are."

Catalina patted Jacob on the back in a friendly way. "I know."

"How did you get Mick to name you vice president?"

Catalina twirled her hair. "Impressed, aren't you, Jakey?"

Jacob laughed. "Yeah, I am."

"Well, you were right. I should be more than just a princess. There are Astrals who still think there should be a royal family, you know. I could have made problems for Mick even if *legally* I wouldn't be a princess. But I told him I wouldn't make any trouble and I'd publicly give up my crown if he named me his vice president."

"Wow," Jacob said. He suddenly felt a little guilty that he had been the one who had prompted her to give up trying to be a princess, the thing she loved the most in the entire universe. But now she could finally decide who she wanted to be instead of just taking the life that was given to her. "That's great, Catalina. Really."

"And who knows," she said with a sly grin. "Maybe Mick isn't the only one in the family who could be president."

"Don't even joke around about that," Jacob said, imagining the look on Mick's face if he lost to his sister. "Because that would be the greatest thing in the history of the universe."

They made their way back to the patio where the others were sitting, and Jacob stuck out his hand to Mick.

"Mr. President," Jacob said.

Mick smiled. "I don't think I'll ever get tired of hearing those words."

"Probably not." Jacob smiled.

Mick turned to Sarah, who still regarded him warily. "I'll never forgive you for kicking me off your campaign," she said.

Mick nodded uncertainly.

"But thanks for doing the right thing and saving Earth," she said.

She punched Mick on the shoulder, which made him immensely happy.

Jacob knew it was time to go. He put his arms around Sarah and Dexter and said, "Shall we?"

"Wait," Mick said.

Jacob, Sarah, and Dexter turned back.

"I'm officially naming you three my Supreme Ambassadors to Earth. President's orders." He gave a lopsided grin. "It's quite a prestigious job, you know."

Jacob laughed. "We'd be honored, Mr. President."

They waved their last good-byes to Catalina and Mick and made their way to Praiseworthy. Jacob couldn't wait to be home at long last, to smell Earth again and be back in his house.

But they had one more stop to make.

chapter 44

The planet was green and moist and covered in tall, beautiful trees. The foliage was dense and full of brilliant and colorful fruits of all varieties, but there was one in particular that was especially common: bananas.

It was a monkey's paradise.

Jacob and Dexter had asked Praiseworthy to research which planet would be the most hospitable for a group of friendly and loyal but not-very-bright space monkeys, and Praiseworthy found one that not only was home to the most varied banana population of any planet in the universe, it was mostly uninhabited and would keep the space monkeys from getting in too much trouble.

At least, unless they started cruising around the galaxy again in their old spaceship.

Jacob watched Dexter walk around with Rufus, excitedly pointing out great things about the new planet, from the sparkling waterfall that would give them perfect water to drink, to all of the different types of fruit, and the many places where he could sleep. Jacob marveled at the way Dexter was so good with the monkeys. He didn't even have any pets, unless you counted his fish, which Jacob had to admit were quite well taken care of.

Sarah sat down in the grass underneath a tall tree and watched Dexter play with the monkeys in their new home.

"Do you think we're going to have to leave Dex here?" she asked.

Jacob laughed. "We might."

Dexter walked back over to Sarah and Dexter holding Rufus's hand, and said quietly, "Rufus has something he wants to say."

Rufus let go of Dexter's hands and scrambled over into Sarah's arms and gave her a big hug.

"Aw," she said. After a little while Rufus let go of Sarah and gave Jacob a hug as well.

"Thanks for messing up Mick's ship," Jacob said.

Rufus started to cling to Dexter, but Dexter shooed him away in such a strong way that Jacob was surprised.

After Rufus walked sadly away, Boris approached the group. He solemnly placed bananas in front of Sarah, Jacob, and Dexter. He looked them over one by one with his brown eyes and then turned and walked away. Jacob supposed that was a moment of appreciation, Boris-style.

Sarah and Jacob stood up, knowing it was just about time to leave. Dexter was staring at the monkeys.

"They'll be all right, Dex," Sarah said.

"We can come visit sometime," Jacob said.

Dexter just nodded. Then he was thrown to the ground as Rufus swooped down from a tree onto his back.

Dexter laughed and cried and gave Rufus one last hug. "You'll be fine, pal," Dexter said.

Rufus stood watching vigilantly as Dexter, Jacob, and Sarah re-boarded Praiseworthy and blasted off into the sky. Dexter waved until he couldn't see any of the monkeys any longer.

The spaceship was very quiet as they flew through space, back through the colorful space kapow detour, and back to the solar system and toward their planet,

which was still safe and secure and waiting for them, thanks to their heroism.

As they neared Earth, Jacob sat alone in his room aboard Praiseworthy, watching old campaign footage of himself on his Telly. He hadn't won, and the campaign already seemed like a distant dream.

But he was proud.

chapter 45

After Praiseworthy touched down in the forest near the block where all the houses looked the same on a pitch-black night, Jacob thought there was something extra-spooky about the forest. The branches seemed to hang closer and more ominously, and the underbrush clung to them as they trudged through the forest.

When they finally reached the street, the houses seemed shabby and worn, and Jacob wondered if perhaps he hadn't noticed how run-down their street had become just a few years after everything was built.

They turned to each other before they parted, and Jacob stuck out his hand. Sarah and Dexter placed one of their hands on top of Jacob's.

"Space friends forever!" Jacob shouted.

"Space friends forever," Sarah and Dexter repeated, but when he heard their voices, he could tell they thought something was different and perhaps slightly odd as well.

They hugged each other and said they'd see each other in school, and set off in the direction of their different houses.

Jacob tried to remember what he was doing the day he had left so he could pick up where his life had left off as if nothing had happened. He'd have to pretend he hadn't just run for president of the universe and lost, escaped crazed soldiers, and helped save the entire planet. No. He was just a regular kid who played pranks on substitutes and tried to have fun and counted the days until summer vacation.

He reached his home and noted that the wreath on the door looked particularly faded, and he pulled it down, since his mom clearly was never going to notice that it was an eyesore.

He opened the door and walked inside and saw an old lady sitting at his table.

"Who are you?" he blurted out before he could think of being polite.

"Jacob," the old lady whispered. "Is that you?" And

with a sudden chill, Jacob realized there was something eerily familiar about her. She looked kind of like his grandmother, but it wasn't her.

"Who—"

But before Jacob could even finish the question, he realized he knew exactly who it was. It was his mom. It was his mom and she was an old lady.

"Jacob," she whispered, stepping over to him, and Jacob retreated despite himself. It was too much. Why was his mom old?

"It's been fifty years, Jacob. Fifty years."

Jacob suddenly realized they hadn't returned to Earth in a time machine. They had returned by spaceship. Last time the king had sent them back so that no time had elapsed, and this time around it hadn't even occurred to them that they should go back the same way.

"I'm so glad to see you," she said in a hoarse voice.

But he was always able to travel around planets without a time problem, so why had fifty years passed on Earth?

"This must be a shock to you." She reached out to him with bony fingers, and he didn't have anywhere else to retreat. His back was against the door. She grasped him by the shoulder and he wanted to scream.

"Jacob, listen to me." She implored him with her

eyes, which were a bit more mottled but were still the eyes that had comforted him so many times when he was a child. He didn't scream and managed to just breathe nervously.

"You must listen to me," she said.

She squeezed his shoulder, and he braced himself for what she was about to say.

"You have to find your father."

ACKNOWLEDGMENTS

JACOB WONDERBAR FOR PRESIDENT OF THE UNIVERSE wouldn't have been possible without my amazing campaign team.

CHIEFS OF STAFF: I don't know where I'd be without the wise council of my agent, Catherine Drayton, and the inspired guidance of Kate Harrison, my editor.

CAMPAIGN MANAGERS: Thanks to Heather Alexander, Patricia Burke, Lyndsey Blessing, Alexis Hurley, Nathaniel Jacks, and Charlie Olson for their hard work making JACOB WONDERBAR happen.

MINISTRY OF CAFFEINE: Special thanks to Philz Coffee of San Francisco for their generous support and for the inspiration provided by Jacob's Wonderbar brew.

CAMPAIGN ART: Thanks to Christopher S. Jennings (illustrations), Jasmin Rubero (interior), and Greg Stadnyk (cover) for bringing Wonderbar to life.

FIELD CREW: I'm immensely grateful for the support of the best friends in the universe. Thanks to Egya Appiah, Justin Berkman, Lisa Brackmann, Holly Burns, Jess Dang, Christian DiCarlo, Dan Goldstein, Jennifer Hubbard, Matt Lasner, Sommer Leigh, Tahereh Mafi, Sarah McCarry, Bryan Russell, Karen Schennum, Sean Slinsky, Jenn Tang, Meg Wilkinson, my blog readers and forumites, and all of my friends at CNET.

FIRST FAMILY: I couldn't have done this without Mom, Dad, Darcie, Scott, and Beth backing me every step of the way.